THE GREEK DEMANDS HIS HEIR

THE GREEK DEMANDS HIS HEIR

BY

LYNNE GRAHAM

First published in Great Britain 2015
by Mills & Boon, an imprint of Harlequin (UK) Limited,
Large Print edition 2015
Eton House, 18-24 Paradise Road,
Richmond, Surrey, TW9 1SR

ISBN: 978-0-263-25703-8

Harlequin (UK) Limited's policy is to use papers that are natural, renewable and recyclable products and made from wood grown in sustainable forests. The logging and manufacturing processes conform to the legal environmental regulations of the country of origin.

Printed and bound in Great Britain
by CPI Antony Rowe, Chippenham, Wiltshire

CHAPTER ONE

'OH, YES, I should mention that last week I ran into your future father-in-law, Rodas,' Anatole Zikos said towards the end of the congratulatory phone call he had made to his son. 'He seemed a little twitchy about when you might…*finally*…be setting a date for the wedding. It has been three years, Leo. When are you planning to marry Marina?'

'She's meeting me for lunch today,' Leo divulged with some amusement, unperturbed by the hint of censure in his father's deep voice. 'Neither of us has any desire to sprint to the altar.'

'After three years, believe me, nobody will accuse you of sprinting,' Anatole said drily. 'Are you sure you *want* to marry the girl?'

Leo Zikos frowned, level black brows lifting in surprise. 'Of course I do—'

'I mean, it's not as if you *need* Kouros Electronics these days.'

Leo stiffened. 'It's not a matter of need. It's a matter of common sense. Marina will make me the perfect wife.'

'There is no such thing as a perfect wife, Leo.'

Thinking of his late and much-lamented mother, Leo clamped his wide sensual mouth firmly closed lest he say something he would regret, something that would shatter the closer relationship he had since attained with the older man. A wise man did not continually look back to a better-forgotten past, he reminded himself grimly, and Leo's childhood in a deeply troubled and unhappy family home definitely fell into that category.

At the other end of the silent line, Anatole made a soft sound of frustration. 'I want you to be happy in your marriage,' he admitted heavily.

'I will be,' Leo told his father with supreme assurance and he came off the phone smiling.

Life was good, in fact life was *very* good, Leo acknowledged with the slow-burning smile on his lean, darkly handsome face that many women found irresistible. He had just that morning closed a deal that had enriched him by millions, hence his father's phone call. His father was quite correct in assuming that Leo did not need to marry Marina simply to inherit her father's electronics company as a dowry. But then Leo had never wanted to marry Marina for her money.

At eighteen, a veteran of the wretched warfare between his ill-matched parents, Leo had drawn up a checklist of the attributes his future wife should have. Marina Kouros ticked literally every box. She was wealthy, beautiful and intelligent as well as being a product of the same exclusive upbringing he had enjoyed himself. They had a great deal in common but they were neither in love nor possessive of each other. Objectives like harmony and practicality would illuminate their shared future rather than dangerous passion and horrendous emotional storms. There would be no nasty surprises along the way with Marina, a young woman Leo had first met in nursery school.

It was forgivable for him to feel just a little self-satisfied, Leo reasoned as his limo dropped him off at the marina in the French Riviera where his yacht awaited him. Exuding quiet contentment, he boarded *Hellenic Lady,* one of the largest yachts in the world. He had made his first billion by the age of twenty-five and five years on he was enjoying life as never before while at the same time ensuring that, although the cutthroat ambiance of the business world was where he thrived, he still took time off to recuperate after working eighteen-hour days for weeks on end.

'Good to have you on board again, sir,' his English captain assured him. 'Miss Kouros is waiting for you in the saloon.'

Marina was scrutinising a painting he had recently bought. A tall slender brunette with an innate elegance he had always admired, his fiancée spun round to greet him with a smile.

'I was surprised to get your text,' Leo confided, giving her a light kiss on the cheek in greeting. 'What are you doing in this neck of the woods?'

'I'm on the way to a country house weekend with friends,' Marina clarified. 'I thought it was time we touched base. I believe my father has been throwing out wedding hints—'

'News travels fast,' Leo commented wryly. 'Apparently your father is becoming a little impatient.'

Marina wrinkled her nose and strolled restively across the spacious room. 'He has his reasons. I suppose I should admit that I've been a little indiscreet of late,' she remarked with a careless shrug of a silk-clad shoulder.

'In what way?' Leo prompted.

'I thought we agreed that until we got married we wouldn't owe each other any explanations,' Marina reminded him reprovingly.

'We may have agreed to go our separate ways until marriage forces us to settle down,' Leo agreed, 'but, as your fiancé, I think I have the right to know what you mean by "indiscreet".'

Marina shot him a bright angry glance. 'Oh, Leo, don't be tiresome! It's not as if you *care*. It's not as if you love me or anything like that!'

Leo remained silent, having long since learnt that listening was by far the best tool to use to calm Marina's quick temper and draw her out.

'Oh, all right!' Marina snapped with poor grace, tossing her silk scarf down on a luxurious sofa in a petulant gesture. 'I've been having a hot affair...and there's been some talk, for which I'm very sorry, but, really, how am I supposed to stop people from gossiping about me?'

His broad shoulders squared below his exquisitely tailored jacket. 'How hot is hot?' he asked mildly.

Marina rolled her eyes and burst out laughing. 'You don't have an atom of jealousy in your entire body, do you?'

'No, but I'd still like to know what's got your father so riled up that he wants us to immediately set a wedding date.'

Marina pulled a face. 'Well, if you must know, my lover is a married man...'

Leo's stunning clean-cut bone structure tautened almost infinitesimally, his very dark eyes shaded by lush black lashes narrowing. He was taken aback and disappointed in her. Adultery was never acceptable in Leo's book and he had made the fatal mistake of assuming that Marina shared that moral outlook. As a child he had lived with the consequences of his father's long-running affair for too many years to condone extra-marital relations. It was the only inhibition he had in the sex department: he would never ever get involved with a married woman.

'Oh, for goodness' sake, Leo!' Marina chided, her face colouring now with angry defensiveness in receipt of his telling silence. 'These things always burn out—you know that as well as I do!'

'I won't pretend to approve. Furthermore that kind of entanglement will damage your reputation…and therefore mine,' Leo reproved coolly.

'I could say that about the little lap-dancer you were sailing round the Med with last summer. You could hardly describe that slutty little baggage as adding lustre to your sophisticated image!' Marina remarked cuttingly.

Predictably, Leo did not even wince, but she flushed uncomfortably at the look he shot her. But then very few things put Leo Zikos out of countenance and regular sex was as important to him as ordered meals and exercise and indeed rated no higher than either by him. He was a very logical male and he saw no need to explain himself when he and Marina had yet to share a bed. The very fact that they had both chosen to retain the freedom of taking other lovers during their long engagement had convinced them that it would be much more straightforward just to save the sex for when they were married.

There is no such thing as a perfect wife, his father had said only an hour or so earlier, but Leo had not expected to be presented with the definitive proof of that statement quite so soon. His high opinion of Marina had been damaged because it was obvious that she saw nothing inherently wrong with sleeping with another woman's husband. Had his own views become so archaic, so unreasonable? Was he guilty of allowing childhood experiences to influence his adult judgement too much? He was well aware that he had friends who engaged in extra-marital affairs, but he would never accept such behaviour from anyone close to him or indeed within his own home.

'I'm sorry but I've had Father on my case. He's not ready to retire and let you take over yet but he's terrified that I'll scare you off,' Marina confided ruefully. 'As I supposedly did with your brother—'

Leo tensed, disliking the reminder that until today Marina's single flaw in his judgement was the reality that she had once enjoyed an ill-judged one-night stand with the younger half-brother whom Leo loathed. That Bastien had treated Marina appallingly in the aftermath was another thing Leo never forgot for, more than anything else, Marina was virtually Leo's best friend and he had always trusted her implicitly.

'Perhaps we should set a wedding date to keep everybody happy,' the brunette suggested wryly.

'I may only be twenty-nine but Father's already getting scared we're getting too old to deliver the grandkids he wants.'

Leo frowned, barely contriving to suppress the need to flinch when she mentioned children. He still wasn't ready to become a father. Parenting required a level of maturity and unselfishness that he was convinced he had yet to attain.

'What about fixing on October for the wedding?' Marina proposed with the sort of cool that implied she had not the faintest idea of his unease. 'I'm no Bridezilla and that would give me three months to make the preparations. I'm thinking of a very boho casual do in London with only family and our closest friends attending.'

They lunched out on deck, catching up on news of mutual friends. It was very civilised and not a single cross word was exchanged. Once Marina had departed, Leo reminded himself soothingly that he had not lost his temper. Even though he had agreed to the wedding date, however, his strong sense of dissatisfaction lingered.

Even worse, that reaction was backed by an even more unexpected feeling, because suddenly Leo was astounded to register that what he truly felt was…*trapped*.

'Nonsense, Grace. Of course you'll go to Turkey with Jenna,' Grace's aunt, Della Donovan, sliced through her niece's protests in her usual brusque and bossy manner. 'A free holiday? Nobody in their right mind would turn their nose up at that!'

Grace gazed out stonily at the pretty garden behind her aunt and uncle's substantial house in north London. Her thoughts were in turmoil because she was trying to come up fast with a polite excuse to avoid the supposed treat of a holiday with her cousin.

'I mean, you've sat all your stupid exams now, haven't you?' her cousin, Jenna, piped up from the leather sofa in the snug beside the kitchen where Grace was seated with Jenna's mother. Mother and daughter were very similar, both of them tall, slender blondes in stark contrast to

Grace, who was small and curvy with a fiery mane of red hair and freckles.

'Yes, but—' Her pale green eyes troubled, Grace bit back the admission that she had been planning to work every possible extra hour at a local bar so that she could save up some money to cushion her when she returned to university at the end of the summer. Any overt reference to her need for financial support was always badly received by her aunt and regarded as being in poor taste. On the other hand, although her aunt was a high-powered lawyer and her uncle a very well-paid business executive, Grace had only ever been given money when she worked for it. From a very early age, Grace had learned the many differences between her standing and Jenna's within the same household.

Jenna had received pocket money while Grace had received a list of household chores to be carried out. It had been explained to her when she was ten years old that she was not their *real* daughter, would never inherit anything from her aunt and uncle and would have to make her own way in adult life. Thus, Jenna had attended a fee-paying school while Grace had attended the comprehensive at the end of the road. Jenna had got her own horse and riding lessons while, in return for the occasional lesson, Grace had got to clean the riding-school stables five days a week after school. Jenna had had birthday parties and sleepovers, which Grace had been denied. Jenna had got to stay on at school, sit her A-levels and go straight to university and at twenty-five years of age worked for a popular fashion magazine. Grace, on the other hand, had had to leave school at sixteen to become a full-time carer for Della's late mother, Mrs Grey, and those years of care and the strain of continuing her studies on a part-time basis had swallowed up what remained of Grace's far from carefree teenage years.

Complete shame at the bitterness of her thoughts flushed Grace's heart-shaped face. She knew she had no right at all to feel bitter because those years of caring for an invalid had been payback to the family who had cared for *her* as a child, she reminded herself sternly. The Donovans, after all, had taken Grace in after her mother's death when nobody else had wanted her. Without her uncle's intervention she would have ended up in the foster-care system and while the Donovans might not have given her love or equality with their own daughter they *had* given her security and the chance to attend a decent school.

So what if she was still the modern-day equivalent of a Victorian charity child or poor relation within their home? That was a comparatively small price to pay for regular meals and a comfortable bedroom, she told herself firmly. She always reminded herself of that truth whenever her uncle's family demanded that she make herself useful, which generally entailed biting her tongue and showing willing even if she didn't *feel* willing. Sometimes though she feared she might explode from the sheer effort required to suppress her temper and watch every word she said.

'Well, then, I suppose I'm going to be stuck

with you,' Jenna lamented, sounding far younger than her years. 'I can hardly go on a girlie holiday alone, can I? And none of my mates can get time off to join me. Believe me, you're my very last choice, Grace.'

Grace compressed her soft full mouth and pushed her rippling fall of fiery hair back from her taut brow where a stress headache was beginning to tighten its grip. Her cousin's best friend, Lola, who had originally planned to accompany Jenna, had broken both legs in a car accident. Sadly that was the only reason that Grace was being invited to take Lola's place and, equally sadly, Grace didn't want to accompany Jenna even though it was a very long time since Grace had enjoyed a holiday.

The unhappy truth was that Jenna didn't like Grace. Jenna had *never* liked Grace and even as adults the cousins avoided spending time together. A much-adored only child, Jenna had thoroughly resented the arrival of another little girl in her home and Grace wasn't even sure she could blame her cousin for her animosity. The

Donovans had hoped that their daughter would see Grace as a little sister, but perhaps the fact that only a year separated the two girls in age had roused competitive instincts in Jenna instead and the situation had only worsened when Grace had unfailingly outshone Jenna in the academic stakes and eventually gone on, in spite of her disrupted education, to study medicine.

'I'm afraid at such short notice Grace is your only option.' Della directed a look of sympathetic understanding at her daughter. 'But I'm sure she'll do her best to be good company.'

Jenna groaned. 'She barely drinks. She doesn't have a boyfriend. She doesn't *do* anything but study. She's like a throwback to the nineteen fifties!'

Della sent Grace an exasperated look. 'You will go with Jenna, won't you?' she pressed. 'I don't want to go to the expense of changing the name on the booking only for you to drop out.'

'I'll go if Jenna really wants me to…' Grace knew when to beat a strategic retreat because crossing Della Donovan was never a good idea.

While she continued to live below the Donovans' roof and paid only a modest amount of rent, Grace knew she had to toe the line in any family crisis, regardless of whether or not it suited her to do so. As a child she had learned the hard way that her compliance was taken for granted and that any kind of refusal or reluctance would be greeted with the kind of shocked reproach that screamed of ingratitude.

For that reason the cash fund she had been hoping to top up to help her through term time would have to take a setback. More worryingly though, could she even hope to still have a job to return to if she took a week off at the height of summer when the bar was busy? Her boss would have to hire a replacement. She suppressed a sigh.

'We're so lucky I thought to renew your passport when I was still hoping to take Mum away for a last holiday…' Della's voice faded and her eyes filmed over at the recollection of her elderly parent's passing.

'I haven't really got any clothes for a beach

holiday,' Grace warned mother and daughter, conscious that Jenna was extremely snobbish about fashion and very conscious of appearances.

'I'll see what I can find you from my cast-offs,' Jenna remarked irritably. 'But I'm not sure my stuff will stretch to your big boobs and even bigger behind. For a wannabe doctor, you're very laid-back about having a healthy body image.'

'I don't think I can fight my natural body shape,' Grace responded with quiet amusement, for she had grown past the stage where Jenna's taunts about her curves could inflict lasting damage. Yes, Grace would very much have liked to be born able to eat anything she liked and remain naturally thin but fate wasn't that kind and Grace had learned to work with what she had and exercise regularly.

A door slammed noisily and Grace came suddenly awake, sitting up with a start and swiftly realising with a sinking heart where she was.

'I am sorry but it is forbidden for people to

sleep here. It is a reception area,' the young woman behind the desk told her apologetically.

Grace threaded unsteady fingers through her tousled mane of hair and rose to her feet, glancing at the clock on the wall with relief. It was after ten in the morning and hopefully she could now return to the apartment she was supposed to be sharing with her cousin.

The blazing row she had had with Jenna late the night before returned to haunt her. So far, the holiday had been a disaster. Possibly it had been rather naïve of Grace to assume that her cousin would not be on a holiday man hunt when she already had a steady boyfriend back home. Unhappily Grace now knew differently. Jenna had only wanted her cousin for company until she found a suitable holiday fling and now that she had found him she simply wanted Grace to vanish. And unfortunately for Grace, Jenna had met Stuart the very first day. He was a banker, loud-spoken and flashy, but her cousin was really keen on him. For the past two nights, Jenna had told Grace that she could not come back to the apartment they were sharing because she wanted to spend the night there with Stuart. Grace had sat up reading in Reception that first night but when Jenna tried to throw her out a second time she had stood her ground and argued.

'I've got nowhere else to go,' she had pointed out to her cousin. 'I don't want to sit up all night in Reception again!'

'If you were halfway normal, you'd have found a man of your own by now!' Jenna had snapped. 'Stuart and I want to be alone.'

'It's a one-room apartment, Jenna. There isn't room for anyone to be alone in a one-room apartment. Couldn't you go back to *his* place tonight?' Grace had dared to suggest.

'He's sharing with a crowd of six blokes. We'd have even less privacy there. In any case, my parents *paid* for our apartment. This is *my* holiday and if it's not convenient for me to have you staying with me, you *have* to get out!' Jenna hissed with a resentful toss of her head.

Recalling that final exchange, Grace grimaced and knocked on the apartment door rather than risk utilising her key because she did not want to interrupt the lovebirds. It was a surprise when Jenna opened the door. Her cousin was already fully dressed and, astonishingly, her blonde cousin smiled at her. 'Come in,' she urged. 'I was just having breakfast. Do you want a cup of tea?'

'I'd kill for a cup.' Grace studied the bathroom door. 'Is Stuart still here?'

'No, he left early. He's off scuba-diving today and I don't know if I'll be seeing him tonight. I thought you and I could go to that new club that's opening up.'

Relieved by Jenna's friendlier attitude while being irritated that Stuart's elusiveness had caused it, Grace nodded. 'If you like.'

Her cousin clattered busily round the tiny kitchen area. 'Stuart wants to cool it…thinks we're moving too far too fast—'

'Oh…' Grace made no further comment, knowing how touchy Jenna could be, confiding in you one moment and snapping your nose off the next.

'There's plenty more fish in the sea!' Jenna declared, slamming the fridge door and straightening, blonde hair flying round her angry face. 'If he comes calling again, he won't find me waiting for him.'

'No,' Grace agreed.

'Maybe you'll meet someone tonight,' her cousin mused. 'I mean, it's past time you leapt off the old virgin wagon and got a life!'

'How do you know I haven't already?' Grace enquired.

'Because you always come home at night and never that late. Know what I think? You're too fussy.'

'Possibly,' Grace conceded, sipping her tea while wondering how soon she could make her excuses, strip off and get into bed to catch up on her sleep.

Jenna's entire world seemed to revolve around the man in her life and she got terribly insecure if she didn't have one. Grace's world, however, revolved round her studies. She had worked incredibly hard to win a place at medical school, was currently at the top of her class and was convinced that men could be a dangerous distraction. Nothing was going to come between Grace and her dream of becoming a really useful person with the medical knowledge and the skills to help others. After all, she had been raised with the warning story of how her mother had screwed up her life by relying on the wrong man.

On the other hand, Grace also knew that sooner or later she would have to find out what sex was all about. How could she possibly advise her future patients if she didn't have that all-important personal experience? But she had yet to meet anyone she wanted to become intimate with and thought it was very sad that something more than logic was required to fuel attraction between a man and a woman. After all, if only logic had ruled, Grace would have become involved with her best friend and study partner, Matt.

Matt was loyal, kind and thoughtful, exactly the sort of man she respected. But if Matt, in his wire-rimmed spectacles and the sweaters his auntie knitted for him, had threatened to take his shirt off she would have run a mile. There was not even the smallest spark on her side of the fence but she kept on trying to feel that spark because she knew that Matt would make a wonderful partner.

Leo stood in the rooftop bar admiring a bird's-eye view of Turunc Bay. By night the busy resort of Marmaris encircled it like a multicoloured jewelled necklace. Flaring scarlet lights in the night sky announced the grand opening of the Fever nightclub. Leo smiled. Rahim, Leo's partner in Fever, knew how to publicise such events and attract the attention of the tourists.

'You've done an amazing job here,' Leo commented approvingly, gazing down through the glass and steel barriers at the packed dance floor.

'Let me give you a *proper* tour,' Rahim urged, keen to show off his masterpiece. A renowned architect and interior designer, he had good reason to want to show off the sleek contemporary lines of his creation. Having delivered exactly what he had promised, Rahim was keen to interest Leo in making another, even larger investment.

Almost a week of solitary introspection on board *Hellenic Lady* had driven Leo to the edge of cabin fever. He was fed up with work, sick of his own company but in no real mood for anyone else's. He strolled down the illuminated staircase with Rahim, his bodyguards surrounding him. The noise of the music was such that he caught only one word in two spoken to him. Rahim was talking about an exclusive hotel complex he wanted to build further along the coast but Leo was not in the right mood to discuss the project. From the landing he gazed down at the crowded floor and that was when he saw her standing by the corner of the brilliantly lit bar, light shining off hair an eye-catching shade of metallic copper…

Her? Just another woman, his brain labelled while his brooding gaze clung to her triangular face. He tore his attention from the fey quality of her delicately pointed features. *Fey?* he silently repeated to himself. Where had he got that strange word from? He noted a lush full pink mouth and the curling mass of glorious red hair snaking down her narrow spine. More red than copper, it also looked natural. His attention lingered, positively drinking in the swooping curves lovingly delineated by a pale lace dress. She had the figure of a fertility goddess with high full breasts, a tiny, highly feminine waist and a voluptuous bottom. His long brown fingers curled round the guard rail, a spooked sensation making the hair rise at the nape of his neck even as the throbbing pulse at his groin reacted and swelled with a very male lack of conscience or morality.

He couldn't remember when he had last been with a woman, an acknowledgement that almost shocked Leo back to reality. Of course, when he was working he would never waste time seeking out a woman…and when he *wasn't*? The necessity of explaining his engagement and specifying no-strings-attached upfront had unequivocally cooled his libido. But now, without the smallest warning, he was recalling Marina's married lover and he was angrily asking himself why he had bothered to halt his high sex drive. After all, Marina didn't care what he did as long as he didn't interfere with her pleasures. And was that truly what he wanted from his future wife? A woman who would never question where he went or what he did? Or demand that he *love* her?

Of course it was what he wanted, he reasoned with growing impatience, particularly when the alternative was jealous, debilitating scenes. Marina's affair had put him on edge but did that affair offend him so much that he intended to break off the engagement and start looking for a more puritanical bride? That would be nonsensical, he decided squarely. He would never know any woman as well as he knew Marina Kouros.

Struggling to suppress his unusually troubled and uneasy thoughts, Leo focused on the redhead's glorious shape. Hunger filled the hollow inside him and it was the sort of hunger he hadn't felt in years, gnawing powerfully at him with painful persistence, ignoring his rigorous efforts to pursue a functional conversation with Rahim. In an abrupt movement of rejection, he looked away from the redhead, but every muscle in his big well-built body snapped taut. Nerves he hadn't known he had jangled like alarm bells until Leo was forced to glance back to the corner of the bar lest he lose sight of the woman. What was it about her? Perhaps he should find out.

In receipt of a chilling glance from Jenna, who was standing at the bar with Stuart, Grace hurriedly turned her head away, colour sparking high over her cheekbones. Stuart had gate-crashed their night out. Jenna had been overjoyed and within minutes of Stuart's appearance had made it clear that Grace was a gooseberry. Clutching the drink that Stuart had insisted on buying her, Grace sipped the sickly sweet concoction and wondered what she was going to do with the rest of her evening. Where was she to go? At least in a crowd she was virtually invisible and attracting no particular attention.

Jenna pushed her way through the crush and settled impatient blue eyes on Grace. 'Why are you still here? I assumed you'd have left by now.'

Grace straightened. 'I'm coming back to the apartment tonight,' she warned her cousin. 'I've spent two nights sitting up in Reception and I'm not doing it again.'

'I can't believe how selfish you're being!' Jenna complained. 'You wouldn't even be having a holiday if it wasn't for me!'

'Change the tune,' Grace advised ruefully, weary of the constant battle to restrain her own nature and simply wanting to be herself. 'The "be grateful, Grace" one is getting old. You asked me on this holiday and I'm afraid you're stuck with me until we go home.'

As Grace averted her attention from her cousin's furious face she noticed a man standing on the stairs watching her. He was drop-dead beautiful, Mr Fantasy in the flesh with black hair, gypsy-gold skin and stunning symmetrical features. He was also tall, broad-shouldered and surprisingly formally clad in a business suit, as were his companions. Somehow, though, she couldn't drag her eyes from him for long enough to scrutinise the other men. His brows were dark and straight, his eyes deep set, glittering in the flickering lights, his nose a classic arch, his mouth a sensual masterpiece.

'*Please* don't come back to the apartment tonight,' Jenna pleaded. 'I haven't got much time left to be with Stuart…'

Stuart lived in London too and Grace marvelled at her cousin's lack of pride. He'd already spelled out the message that he wanted nothing more than a fling. Jenna flung her a last look of angry appeal before turning on her heel to return to Stuart. As Grace turned away, intending to leave the club and find a quiet café where she could read the book in her bag, she almost tripped over the large man in her path.

'Mr Zikos would like you to join him in the VIP section for a drink.'

Involuntarily, Grace raised a brow as she glanced back at the stairs. Mr Zikos? He nodded acknowledgement and suddenly he smiled at her and in the space of a second he went from stunning to downright breathtaking, the clear-cut austere lines of his darkly handsome face slashed by an almost boyish grin that was utterly and incredibly appealing. Later, Grace swore her heart, always the most reliable of organs around men, leapt in her chest and bounced with enthusiasm, leaving her feeling seriously short of breath and oddly dizzy.

A drink? The VIP section? What did she have to lose? A bouncer undid the ceremonial velvet rope cutting off the stairs and Grace unfroze, moving forward with the strangest sense of anticipation.

CHAPTER TWO

LEO EXTENDED A lean tanned hand with unexpected formality. 'Leos Zikos. My friends call me Leo.'

Grace touched his fingers in a glancing collision that made her teeth grit at her own ineptitude. But up close, he was so tall, so dark, so strikingly handsome that he unnerved her and given the smallest chance to scamper back down the short flight of stairs without making a fool of herself she would have fled. 'Grace Donovan,' she supplied a little gruffly, her heart beating very fast in what felt like her throat as she hurriedly sat down on the seat he indicated and nodding belated recognition of the presence of a second, smaller man.

'Irish?' Leo quirked a brow.

'My mother was but I'm from London.'

Leo asked her what she would like to drink.

'Something plain and simple. This...' Grace indicated the glass in her hand with its elaborate green concoction and umbrella with a faint wrinkling of her nose '...is like a sugar bomb.'

After introducing her to Rahim, Leo informed her that they owned the club. Grace told him that she was a student on holiday with her cousin. A waiter arrived with a tray and champagne was served with a flourish. The first waiter was closely followed by two more, who presented plates of delicate little snacks. Leo asked her what music she would like and within the minute the DJ himself was surging upstairs and standing right in front of her while she told him.

At first Grace was entranced by the heady assault of Leo's full attention and she sipped and she nibbled, leaning closer to politely listen to the two men discuss the couples-only complex that Rahim wanted to design. By the time the older man had extracted a plan from an inner pocket along with photos of the site and its superb beach, Grace was getting bored and, what was more, by then her favourite song was playing and she scrambled up off her seat to stand at the rail, her feet shifting in time to the throbbing beat of the music.

'Dance?' she directed hopefully at Leo, who was welded to the spot by the luscious view of her swaying hips.

He grimaced. 'I don't,' he told her without apology, fighting the swelling at his groin.

'No problem,' Grace told him with an easy smile and a glint in her green eyes as she headed back down the stairs to the dance floor. Just for one night, she thought rebelliously, her thoughts still dwelling on Jenna's humiliating attacks, she was going to be herself, her *real* self that she never dared to show at home. And that meant that she would do and say what she wanted, rather than maintaining her usual quiet role in which she worked to politely conform and meet other people's expectations.

Leo was stunned by her departure. There had been no fuss, no drama, just an unobtrusive determination to do as she liked rather than try to please him. She hadn't flirted or flattered either. His straight brows pleated in frank bewilderment. Women didn't behave like that around Leo. Even Marina, who liked her own way, tailored herself to a neat fit of his preferences while in his company.

'I believe you have met a woman with a mind of her own,' Rahim remarked. 'And talking about such women, I am married to one and if I am not home soon, I will be unpopular.'

Leo stood at the rail, broad shoulders straight as an axe blade and rigid with tension until he relocated Grace again. He noted that she was dancing just at the edge of the floor and he wondered if she planned to join him again. Or was she expecting him to chase after her? Leo didn't chase: he had never had to go to that much effort with a woman. Consequently, he should've been irritated by her behaviour but he was not and he didn't understand that.

What was it about her? She had extraordinary eyes, he recalled, as pale and translucent a green as a piece of sea glass he had once picked up off a beach as a boy. And just as the sea fascinated him, she did as well. He was down the stairs before he even knew he was planning to retrieve her.

'Can't...' he informed her with a wry look when she studied him expectantly. 'No sense of rhythm.'

Leo stood there in front of Grace like a very large statue frozen in place. Her breath hitched in her throat as she looked up into his exotically dark eyes, noting the luxuriance of his black lashes. He was gorgeous. Did he really need to dance? a little voice enquired wryly inside her head.

'Anyone can dance,' Grace told him softly.

He bent his arrogant dark head, his big body still infuriatingly rigid in stance. 'I don't do anything that I can't do superlatively well.'

Grace grinned at that Alpha male excuse and planted her hands on his lean hips. *'Move,'* she urged him, amused against her will by his frozen stance. '*Feel* the beat...'

The only thing Leo felt as she tugged him to

her to demonstrate that elusive rhythm was the punch of lust that almost left him light-headed as he looked down into her laughing sea-glass eyes. Women didn't ever laugh *at* Leo. They laughed *with* him. He shifted his lean hips in response to her guidance, but only to take advantage of the opportunity to yank her closer and line up that teasing, tantalising mouth of hers with his own.

In the space of a heartbeat, Grace travelled from amusement to another place entirely and it was a shockingly unfamiliar place. She had no experience of passion and suddenly there it was, shamelessly smashing down her defences and powered solely by the hungry, scorching demand of his mouth. For a split second she stiffened in shock and then she turned boneless, liquid heat rolling through her veins. His tongue plundered the semi-closed seam of her lips and she parted them for him, head falling back on her shoulders as he took immediate advantage. He plundered the moist, tender interior of her mouth with an acute sense of the rhythm he had denied, sending an electrifying shudder of piercing sexual pleasure travelling through her.

Leo lifted his head, closed a hand firmly over hers and urged her back up the stairs. Grace blinked like a sleepwalker suddenly forced awake, astonishment rising inside her that a man could actually make her feel like that…all shaky and molten and needy, her nipples tight and aching, warmth and dampness gathering between her thighs. Her own response was a revelation to her. Yes, he did kiss superlatively well, she acknowledged dizzily, and didn't that make him the perfect man for her sexual experiment? Presumably if he was that good at kissing he would be reasonably proficient at the rest of it as well.

'Another drink?' Leo proffered the glass and extended the snacks, willing to do just about anything to ensure that he was able to keep his hands off her for long enough to get back in control of his unruly body. Leo did not like to lose control but he was still hard and throbbing almost painfully, his libido all too eager to continue what he had begun. But haste wasn't cool and Leo was never hasty. He didn't do one-night stands either, at least not since he was a teenager. But Grace drew him like a bee to a hive of honey.

Grace clasped the champagne flute gratefully in one hand, astounded to realise that her hand was trembling slightly. But then it wasn't really Leo still having that effect on her, she told herself urgently, it was more probably the distinctly daunting knowledge that she had decided that, given the opportunity, she would make love with the man she was with. She glanced uncertainly up at him, her gaze drinking in the height and slant of his cheekbones, the strong angular jut of his classic nose, the mobile expressiveness of his wide, sculpted mouth. He was absolutely beautiful in the way only a very masculine man could be without the smallest hint of prettiness, although the jury was still out when it came to the ridiculous length of the long curling black lashes framing his remarkable eyes.

'Are you single?' she checked a tad abruptly.

'Yes. Will you spend the night with me?' Leo

murmured sibilantly, his accent underscoring the syllables with a rasping edge. 'I've never wanted a woman as much as I wanted you on that floor.'

His directness disconcerted Grace but pleased her as well because she valued candour. She laughed. 'It's all right. You don't have to say stuff like that. I made up my mind to say yes when you kissed me.'

It would be a completely *practical* sexual experiment, Grace reasoned nervously, striving to reassure herself about a spontaneous decision that was unusual for her. Here she was far from home and she would never see him again, so there would be no lingering embarrassment, no further meetings, and no lasting connection. She had always believed in calling a spade a spade and the two of them were both after the same thing: a complication-free hook-up. He was as close to perfect for her purposes as it was possible to get.

Relief gripping him at her immediate agreement shorn of any prevarication, Leo closed a powerful arm round her narrow waist and gazed down at her with an intense sense of satisfaction and anticipation. Her nose turned up a little at the end and there was a scattering of freckles across the bridge but he discovered that he found those flaws endearing rather than noticeable deficiencies. 'It *wasn't* flattery.'

'If you say so,' Grace fielded, unconvinced, utterly challenged by the concept that she had sufficient sex appeal to tax the restraint of so sophisticated and good-looking a male. 'But outside a serious relationship sex is only a recreational pursuit.'

Taken aback by that prosaic comment and struck by an outlook that came remarkably close to his own, Leo elevated an ebony brow. 'But a most enjoyable one.'

Grace almost hit him with the shocking survey figures on the level of female sexual dysfunction and dissatisfaction in society but decided to keep wannabe-Dr-Grace firmly under restraint. 'I certainly hope so,' she said, her face heating at the very thought of what she had already agreed to do with him. She fretted that alcohol could be affecting her judgement although she had only had two drinks and hadn't finished the first.

But no, she wasn't drunk, not even tipsy because she always got giggly if she drank too much. Yet in retrospect her agreement to spend the night with him seemed so cold-blooded that she agonised over it for a nerve-racked few minutes of insecurity. Yet wasn't that attitude more sensible than waiting in the naïve hope that someone would eventually offer her both romance *and* commitment? She was almost twenty-five years old and she had waited long enough for a man to offer her a picture-book perfect solution to the loneliness she worked hard at hiding from the outside world. It wasn't going to happen in the foreseeable future and she had to be level-headed about her prospects. Matt was a great study mate and friend but sadly not lover material.

In any case she was an intelligent adult woman and free to do as she liked if she found a suitable attractive partner, she reminded herself stubbornly. By tomorrow she would finally know what sex was all about and at least she wouldn't have to spend another night trying to stay awake in the reception back at the apartment block. In truth, even the offer of a bed for the night was ridiculously welcome.

Leo traced a strong brown forefinger along her slim freckled arm, lingering on the fine skin of her wrist. Her skin was very soft and satin smooth and much paler than his own. 'I will please you,' he insisted.

A slight shiver racked Grace as if, after that kiss, her entire body had become super sensitive to his touch. She badly wanted him to kiss her again and the strength of that craving unsettled her. Never until that moment had she appreciated how powerful sexual hunger could be. Oh, she had read about it, heard about it, talked intellectually about it but all of those stories and assumptions were meaningless when set next to the actual experience. Leo Zikos would be like her personal science project, she told herself soothingly, and in the process of her research she would learn much that she needed to know.

She asked Leo when Rahim had left and for a few minutes they discussed the hotel scheme.

'You were getting bored,' Leo commented. 'I should apologise for that.'

'Is your business based on nightclubs?'

'No, this is my only investment in that line. I started out as a corporate trader and built a property empire with my investments. Now I have hotels, mobile phone and transport companies...' Leo shifted a hand to indicate the breadth of his interests with an elegance of movement that was compelling. 'I believe very strongly in diversification. My father once went bust because he concentrated all his energies in one field. What are you studying at university?'

'I'm about to go into my final year.' Grace responded as if she had misheard his question because she was in no hurry to tell him that she was a medical student. More than one male had backtracked from Grace in the past once they had discovered how clever she was. It was surprising how many men were turned off by her high IQ.

She met his riveting dark eyes and discovered that below the lights they weren't really dark at all. They were tawny gold and vibrant with power and a tiny shiver of naked awareness snaked down her taut spinal cord.

Leo stared down at her, a brooding quality tightening his lean dark features. He had read about pheromones and he was wondering if it was possible that she put out some strange invisible chemical message that turned him on hard and fast in a way that seemed to make no sense. After all, even if he was reacting like one, he wasn't a teenager at the mercy of his hormones any more.

He bent his head and the coconut scent of her shampoo filtered appealingly into his nostrils but he wasn't thinking about that when he looked at her ripe pink mouth. He moved nearer, his breath fanning her cheek. Almost imperceptibly she swayed closer. His arms tautened round her and without the smallest forewarning of what he was about to do he devoured the voluptuous promise of her lips with a passionate intensity that sent arousal roaring through him like an out-of-control fire.

The second kiss was even hotter than the first, Grace acknowledged dizzily, and she'd known it was coming, forewarned by the glitter of his eyes, the tensing of his arms round her and the quickened thump of his heartbeat beneath her palm when she was forced to plant a hand against his shirtfront to retain her balance on the edge of the seat. She had no thought of avoiding that kiss. In fact, excitement was zinging through her as an astonishing surge of awareness travelled through every nerve ending in her body, super-sizing her every response.

Leo dragged his mouth from hers with the greatest of difficulty. 'Let's go,' he husked.

She had only been with him a little over an hour, Grace acknowledged in dismay. I'm a slut, I'm a slut, she reflected in mortification. Maybe sometimes sluts have more fun, said another voice inside her head and she almost laughed, registering that she was on a kind of mindless adrenalin high as if she had just reached the top of a ski run. She looked up at him, her gaze skimming over the already familiar lines of his breathtakingly handsome face and her tummy turning over even as heat leapt through her lower body in a disturbing wave of reaction. 'Go where?'

'Back to my yacht,' Leo advanced, urging her to her feet while carefully avoiding the scrutiny of his bodyguards. Making out with an audience was not cool and he had never done it before. What was he? A hot-under-the-collar kid? A dark flush had scored his strong cheekbones.

'You're here on a yacht?' Grace frowned, surprised by the news.

'I've been cruising the Med for the past week.' Leo walked her down the stairs, but not before one of the men seated at the table across the way cleared their path. When she turned her head she saw the other two falling into step behind them. One of them was talking into one of those security earpieces she had only previously seen worn in films and the men backed into the dancers to impose a barrier around her and Leo and ensure their smooth passage across the crowded dance floor.

'Are those men bouncers?' she asked.

'My security team.'

'Why do you need a security team?' Grace enquired nervously.

'Protection. I've had a security presence in my life since childhood,' Leo confided evenly, as if it was the most normal thing in the world. 'My mother and her sister were Greek heiresses. Sadly, my aunt was kidnapped and held for ransom as a teenager.'

'Good grief,' Grace whispered in the comparative quiet of the club foyer. 'Was she freed? I mean, did she come home again?'

'Yes, she came home but she never fully recovered from her ordeal,' Leo replied grimly.

Grace stiffened, registering that something pretty horrible had happened to his aunt while she was being held and she suppressed a shiver.

'It makes more sense to guard against such risks,' Leo declared in a lighter tone as a car drew up by the kerb and one of his guards hastened to open the door for them.

Grace was nonplussed, out of her depth and feeling it. He had to be very rich to feel the need to take such precautions. She was with a man who inhabited a totally different world from her own and she breathed in slow and deep while she wondered if she had made a rather foolish decision.

'This is a little unnerving for me,' Grace admitted abruptly, watching one man climb in the front with the driver while the others climbed into the second car behind them.

'Ignore them…I do,' Leo asserted, recognising that she was not impressed like most women but instead ill at ease with the trappings of his lifestyle.

On the drive to the marina, her breath feathered in her throat while Leo chatted easily about his recent travels and stroked the back of her hand with a lazy forefinger. The car stopped and the passenger door sprang open. In her high heels, his hand cupping her elbow to steady her, she walked a few steps and stopped dead when Leo stepped into a motorboat and extended his hand to her.

'I… I… Where's your boat?' Grace demanded uneasily.

'There…'

Grace followed his gesture and further out in the bay saw a ship's silhouette etched against the moonlit sky. 'It looks like the *Titanic*!' she gasped because it was huge.

'An unfortunate comparison. I can assure you that *Hellenic Lady* is seaworthy and safe.' Leo stepped back onto the marina and bent down to scoop her up into his arms before stepping back into the launch with her.

He had acted so fast Grace hadn't had a moment to do more than utter a startled squeak of protest. Then he set her down again, settling her into a padded seat by his side. The speedboat was racing across the sea before she could even catch her breath. A night on a yacht, she thought ruefully. Well, that might be fun, she conceded, and fun had been in very short supply since she'd arrived in Marmaris as Jenna's pretty much unwelcome guest.

'OK?' Leo prompted as the launch reached the yacht.

'I'm fine.' Grace swallowed back her worries and allowed him to guide her up a gangway.

Leo didn't know what had come over him. He wasn't the caveman type but as soon as he had seen her anxious expression he had panicked, deeply unaccustomed at the idea that she might be changing her mind, and he had snatched her off the marina and got her into the launch as fast as he could. Grace Donovan brought out something in him that he didn't like, something very basic and elemental and essentially…unnerving. Possibly once he figured out what that mystery something was he would feel better about it.

A man in a peaked cap greeted Leo, and Grace didn't know where to look because she was embarrassed, convinced that their plans for what remained of the night had to be obvious. Leo wafted her away up another staircase and down a corridor. He spread open the heavy carved doors and invited her to precede him.

Her sea-glass eyes widened to their fullest extent, stunned appreciation etched on her lovely face as she slowly executed a circle to take in the full effect of the gorgeous bedroom. Huge windows looked out on the starry sky and the dark rippling water so far below. Leo hit a button and blinds buzzed into place to seal them into privacy. Blinking, she turned, eyes skating hastily over the opulent bed with its perfectly draped oyster silk spread. There were paintings on the walls, honest-to-goodness oil paintings, at least one of which looked sufficiently classic and imposing enough to be an Old Master.

'Would you like a drink? Something to eat?' Leo enquired, wondering why he had brought her to the master suite when he usually took his lovers to one of the guest cabins for the night. He had always been a very private man.

'No, thanks. I'm sorry, I'm a bit out of my depth with all this,' Grace confessed, hands shifting to shyly indicate the unbelievable luxury of her surroundings.

And yet she looked as if she belonged, Leo thought suddenly, her hair a river of fire across her shoulders, framing her astonishingly vivid little face, light green eyes flickering with uncertainty against a pallor that only made her freckles stand out. She truly was a beauty in a very natural way that was entirely new to a male much more accustomed to women groomed to a high standard of artificial perfection.

'It's only money.'

'Only someone with pots of it would say that,' Grace quipped, straightening her slim shoulders. 'We're from very different backgrounds, Leo.'

'There are no barriers here.' Leo stalked closer, surprisingly light and quiet on his feet for so large a male. He reached for her hand and drew her towards him. 'I wasn't exaggerating when I told you how much I wanted you, *meli mou*.'

'What did you call me?'

'Meli mou?' His mouth quirked as he brushed a stray red strand of hair back off her cheekbone.

Her hair felt like silk against his fingers and she was much smaller than his women usually were, the top of her head barely reaching his shoulder in spite of her fantastically high heels. Her diminutive stature gave him the oddest protective feeling. 'It's Greek for "my honey".'

'I'm more tart than sweet,' Grace warned him.

'Sugar cloys,' Leo husked and he wondered if that was the very basic truth that explained his reaction to her. She was independent and outspoken and he had never met anyone quite like her before.

He stroked a finger across the pulse flickering madly at her collarbone and her breath tripped in her throat. 'You keep touching me…'

His eyes glowed potent gold. 'I can't keep my hands off you. Is it a problem?'

Grace's lashes screened her eyes. She wasn't used to being touched and he did it with such ease and spontaneity. Her mother had been physically demonstrative, when she had been sober, and their brief time at the commune in Wales had been almost happy. But, after her mother's death, her uncle's family had been much more reserved and Grace had received little physical affection from them. 'No, not a problem,' she said in a low voice, thinking she had better watch herself with him because somehow he was getting under her skin in a way she had not foreseen.

'*Thee mou*, it is as well because I'm not sure I could stop.' Leo slid off his jacket and tossed it on a nearby chair, a lean brown hand tugging roughly at the knot on his silk tie and casting it aside.

I'm only with him to have sex, to lose my virginity and gain a little experience, Grace reminded herself doggedly. No other feelings should enter the equation. If she kept it simple and straightforward, she wouldn't get hurt as her mother had been hurt, putting her future in a man's hands and learning her mistake too late. She had only been a little girl when she had first found out about her father's betrayal but the memory of her mother's pain had lingered.

'Hey…' Leo turned her head back to him to

stare down into her haunted eyes. 'Where did you go just now? Bad memories?'

Grace reddened with chagrin. 'Something like that…'

'Another man?' Leo gritted, appalled by the rage that flooded him at the idea that she might be thinking of a lost lover while she was with him.

'Not that it's any of your business, but no,' Grace countered succinctly, lifting her chin. 'I don't allow men to screw with my mind.'

'Only your body?' Leo breathed, reaching for both her hands to tug her to him.

Her copper lashes lowered and she glanced up at him from beneath their spiralling cover. 'Only my body. I hope that's a deal?'

'We're talking too much,' Leo gritted, on fire from that provocative upward glance of hers, scarcely able to credit that *she* was warning *him* off wanting anything more than sex. Wasn't that his line? Hadn't that always been *his* line? It made him feel curiously insecure, not a sensation he enjoyed.

His mouth enveloped hers again and the piercingly sweet thrust of his tongue made her shudder, heat surging up from her pelvis, sending fingers of flame to make her nipples tingle and swell.

'I'm going to undress you very, very slowly…' Leo asserted, 'revealing only one tiny piece of you at a time.'

Her tummy performed a somersault, consternation filling her as she wondered if she would be up to that sophisticated challenge.

CHAPTER THREE

LEO'S LIPS WERE aggressive and smooth on Grace's as he lifted her and laid her down gently on the bed, breaking contact only to flip off her shoes and let them fall.

Grace breathed in deep, mastering her nervous tension, terrified of letting it show. Of course she could have told him the truth that she was a newbie in the bedroom, but she was convinced that it would seriously dent her desirability in his eyes. And being treated as if she were rather more beautiful and seductive than she was felt especially good to her at that moment. She wondered where the bathroom was, knew she would have preferred diving in there to undress before reappearing casually wrapped in a towel or something. But wouldn't that be aping a fifties bride on her wedding night? Shyness and inhibitions were not sexy, she told herself impatiently.

'I love your hair,' he told her, stroking the tumbled strands as he sank down on the bed at the same time as he removed his cufflinks and unbuttoned his shirt. 'It's a gorgeous colour.'

'I got called "Carrots" at school and hated it for years,' Grace recalled with a rueful grin.

'When you smile, *meli mou*, your whole face lights up,' Leo said softly, lowering his head to claim another passionate kiss that rocked her even where she lay, her body behaving like a Geiger counter detecting radiation, strange new reactions awakening inside her.

His shirt parted, giving her a glimpse of broad, strong pectoral muscles and washboard abs that made her mouth run dry. He was excessively good to look at, what one of her friends would term 'man candy'. The pool of warmth at her pelvis spread. He turned her over, ran down the zip and gently spread the edges back, kissing one slim white freckled shoulder and then the other and tugging her back against him.

'Do you always go this slow?'

No, he didn't and, considering that he was already hugely aroused, Leo had no idea why he was determined to be the perfect lover for her. 'Depends on my mood… I want to savour you…'

He slid the sleeves down her arms and paused to appreciate the full globes filling the cups of her bra before he succumbed to temptation. With a soft little sound of impatience, he snapped loose the catch on the bra and raised his hands to cradle her superb breasts, massaging the creamy flesh, pressing her flat to explore them with his mouth and lingering over her straining rosy nipples.

'You have amazing breasts,' Leo muttered thickly as he dallied there, employing both his tongue and the glancing edge of his teeth to tease the straining buds.

Grace was rather more amazed at the effect he was having on her ignorant body. A hungry ache stirred at the heart of her. All of a sudden catching her breath was a challenge and she ran her fingers through his luxuriant black hair, surprised by how soft it was and how right it felt to touch him. She had thought she might have to steel herself to respond to him, genuinely hadn't expected to be quite so caught up in the process as she was, had even believed that throughout the process some part of her quick and clever brain would be standing back assessing and judging. Instead as he lifted her to find her mouth again Grace was engaging in some exploration of her own, hands sliding below the open shirt to trace his wonderfully honed muscular torso, skimming over the flat male nipples and the etching of crisp dark hair sprinkled there before sliding down to stroke the flexing muscles of his taut stomach.

'*Don't*...not this first time,' Leo urged, pulling back from her to slide off the bed. 'I'm too close to the edge.'

Grace blinked, bemused, having assumed he would be as eager to be touched as she was. And, 'not this *first* time'? Was that simply his prodigious self-assurance doing the talking for him? Her body all aquiver about even the thought of a single experience and the unlikelihood of her wanting a second, Grace watched him strip off his clothing with something less than the laid-back cool she had come to expect from him.

Everything came off at once, ensuring that she had little time to be curious about what her first aroused male looked like. He was larger than she had assumed he would be, but that was only a point of academic interest, she assured herself nervously, surveying the prodding length and breadth of his bold shaft. She knew she would stretch and she envisaged neither pain nor anything else that might reveal her inexperience. After all she had gone horse riding from an early age and believed any physical barrier would be long gone. With the same focused intellectual interest, Grace wondered why she literally felt overheated when she looked at Leo naked, her body hot, her breath catching in her throat as if she lacked oxygen.

'You're very quiet,' Leo remarked, coming back down to her, dropping several foil-wrapped contraceptives on the bedside cabinet, soothing

Grace's instinctive terror of what had happened to her mother also happening to her.

For a split second she was almost tempted to tell him the truth about herself but innate reserve, learned growing up in a household where she had never belonged, kept her silent.

'I'm used to women who chatter,' Leo admitted with a slanting grin that was irresistible.

'I'm quiet,' Grace admitted, sliding for purchase on the slippery surface of the bedspread and flipping it back to scramble beneath the sheets, still clad in her panties, which she whisked off under cover.

'Someone so beautiful could never be shy,' Leo assumed, sliding in beside her in one lithe movement to reach for her. 'But you are a cheat… I wanted to see you…*all* of you.'

Grace knew she wasn't beautiful. She had grown up with the belief that tall, thin and blonde was the epitome of beauty and all the most popular girls at school had fitted that blueprint. But when Leo studied her with wide wondering eyes she felt beautiful for the first time in her life and, even though she was convinced it wasn't true, it made her feel special. 'I have to admit I liked seeing you,' she confessed tensely, striving to reward his appreciation.

'Really?' Leo laughed, amused by that little morsel of flattery when he was accustomed to a positive barrage of compliments in the bedroom. He admired Grace's restraint and lack of drama even while he could hardly wait to shatter her defences and see her lose herself in the throes of passion.

He kissed her and it was like the first time all over again, his tongue thrusting into her mouth to set her alight, tiny little spasms of excitement igniting afresh to clench her womb. He pushed her legs apart, ran a forefinger along the seam there and she stiffened, knowing she was damp and knowing it was absolutely crazy to get into bed with him and be embarrassed about such a natural thing but unable to overcome her self-consciousness. What on earth had happened to her belief that she could make him a science project? she asked herself suddenly, dismayed to be losing her detachment. She closed her eyes tight while he played with the most sensitive spot on her entire body, pleasure and longing traversing her in steady waves. She gritted her teeth, suddenly terrified of getting too carried away and losing control as her hips rose involuntarily.

She made no effort to evade him when he pushed back the sheet. In fact she braced herself to tolerate the intimacy as he tipped her legs over his shoulders and homed in on the most private part of her.

'You're beautiful here too,' Leo purred with a lack of inhibition that shook her and she studied the ceiling in disbelief, struggling to retain some distance from the leaps and jerks of her feverishly aroused body. Then the tip of his tongue touched her and circled her and a rolling wave of pleasure gripped her. Her eyes closed, teeth tightening to hold back a gasp but her control was broken within moments because she had never ever experienced that much pleasure. Sounds were wrenched from her parted lips and her fingers knotted in his hair as the screaming ache for fulfilment inside her built and built and she was lost in the storm of it with her heart thundering and her body writhing. And when she reached a climax, it *was* explosive and mind-blowing and all the superlative exaggerated words of description that once would have made her roll her eyes in disbelief.

'You're incredibly responsive, *meli mou*,' Leo husked, finding his every expectation mirrored in the dazed pleasure in her wide eyes and the closing of her arms round him in the aftermath.

Grace was dimly aware of him reaching for a foil packet. Her body might still be leaping with pleasure but her brain was firing back on all cylinders because he had blown *her* expectations out of the water with his very first move.

He shifted over her, lithe and confident as a jungle cat on the hunt, and she shut her eyes tight again against the intrusion of his. It was going to happen, it was *finally* going to happen and she would be like almost every other woman, no longer in the dark, no longer ignorant. But it had never occurred to her before that any man could make her want him so desperately that nothing else seemed to matter. His hands cupped her hips to tilt her boneless body back into a better position and then she felt the crown of him at her entrance and she tensed at the exact same moment he thrust deep and hard. The tender tissue of her channel burned and then a sharp little sting sliced through her, provoking a cry of discomfort from her lips. Leo froze.

'What the hell…? I *hurt* you?'

Forced by the unexpected to open her eyes, Grace knew her face had to be redder than a ripe apple. 'I was a virgin,' she admitted belatedly.

'A *virgin*?' Leo yelled, as if she had jabbed him with a red-hot poker. 'And you're telling me that *now*?'

'It was private,' Grace told him succinctly, her lush mouth folding into a compressed line. 'Now that it's done, can we just go back to where we were?'

Go back to where we were? In a different mood, Leo would have laughed at that wording. But he was in the grip of angry astonishment, his every assumption about her wiped out. He didn't like surprises, but as Grace shifted up to him in reminder that he was still inside her he discovered that his body was much less particular. He stared down at her with stunning dark golden eyes. He was her first and there was something mysteriously satisfying about that discovery. She was so tight and warm and wet. Struggling to control his every move, he sank deeper and a breathy little sigh that certainly wasn't a complaint escaped her.

Grace shut her eyes again, ripples of pleasure reclaiming her, that momentary stab of discomfort forgotten. She could feel his girth stretching her and his hips ground into hers with every slow, heavy thrust. He was being *so* careful.

'It's OK…you're not hurting me at all,' she mumbled guiltily.

His pace quickened and a deep guttural moan was torn from him as her body clenched around his. He felt so good Grace couldn't believe it, couldn't believe she had lived so many years without realising what she was missing out on.

A sense of wonder seized her while her heart rate began to race with enjoyment as he pushed into her harder, faster and deeper. She couldn't speak, she couldn't breathe for excitement; she felt as though she had stolen a ride on a comet. The excitement rose and rose to breaking point when without her volition her body jerked into another intense orgasm. Ecstatic cries broke from her lips as the white-hot heat exploded in her pelvis and left her lying limp and utterly drained but with a glorious feeling of satisfaction that was new to her.

'Care to tell me why?' Leo demanded, shattering her idyll. 'Why did you pick me?'

'You did the picking,' Grace reminded him without hesitation, lifting her arms to break his hold on her to enable her to roll away. 'There's no agenda here, if that's what is worrying you. I found you attractive and I decided it was time that I took the plunge.'

'I would have preferred a warning,' Leo told her drily.

'I wasn't expecting that jab of pain. After years

of horse riding I assumed there'd be nothing there…my mistake,' Grace pronounced with dignity. 'But thanks for the experience. You were very good.'

Prior to his engagement, Leo had been a legendary womaniser but he felt quite ridiculously put down by Grace's comment. He sprang off the bed and then a much more pressing matter came to his attention before he could reach the bathroom and he uttered a single crude expletive.

Grace froze at the sound of that word. When she was a child she hadn't known it was a bad word because her mother had used it all the time. Unhappily when she had used that word in Jenna's home, her aunt had screamed at her and put a soap bar in her mouth. She had still been throwing up when her uncle came home. The couple had had a massive row and Grace had never ever used that word again.

Impervious to her reaction, Leo had strode into the bathroom to dispose of the evidence.

He reappeared, bronzed and stark naked in the doorway. 'The condom broke…'

Grace sat up in horror. 'What?'

'Breaking you in probably strained it,' Leo retorted with deliberate curtness because it was just one more unexpected development that he didn't want.

'It…*burst*?' Grace whispered. 'But I'm not on the pill—'

Leo grew even more rigid in his bearing. 'Shouldn't you have taken that precaution before you embarked on a one-night stand?'

Grace just ignored him; she didn't have to talk to him just because she had slept with him. In fact now that the main event was over she decided that she should ask for a boat back to the marina. Or would that be running away?

'May I use the bathroom?' she asked with careful politeness. 'And then possibly you could organise me a lift back to the marina?'

Leo moved to let her into the bathroom but his temper was now on a short fuse. Wham, bam, thank you, sir. Well, a woman had never treated him like that before but there was always a first time and maybe that was healthy for his ego. But the recollection that it had been *her* first time stopped his building aggression in its tracks. She didn't know what she was doing. She wasn't as much quiet as she was secretive and, flipping mentally back through the time he had been with her, he reckoned she had to be as innocent as a newborn lamb when it came to the nastier things in life. Perspiration beaded his upper lip when he thought of what might have happened to Grace had she gone off so casually and trustingly with some of the seedier individuals he had met on his travels.

'I want you to stay the night. I'll take you back tomorrow,' he stated.

'This is a one-night stand…you don't get to tell me what to do!' Grace flamed back at him with spirit.

'You're not doing so well right now when it comes to looking after yourself,' Leo pronounced drily.

In the space of a moment, Grace travelled from

a mood of silent resentment to one of raging rancour and sooner than betray herself by spitting out something inappropriate, she slammed the bathroom door on him. Who did he think would look after her but her own self if she was unlucky enough to conceive after that contraceptive accident? It was none of his business that she had come on holiday without planning to have sex with anyone and she wasn't taking the pill because she hadn't wanted to bombard her body with hormones before she was even sexually active. On the other hand, should she have foreseen the possibility that she might suddenly change her mind as she had done this very evening? Grace stood below the shower in a daze counting the days of her cycle, soon realising that the condom could not have failed at a worse time.

Leo swore vehemently beneath his breath and went off to use another shower. Why was she angry with him? Accidents happened, although it was the first time he had found himself in such a situation. Even as a teenager, Leo had never had unprotected sex because he knew all too well the cost of such carelessness. His half-brother's birth to his father's mistress had been a painful lifelong commitment for Anatole Zikos *and* his wife and son.

Grace emerged from the bathroom wrapped in the white towelling robe she had found hanging there. It was huge on her but she had rolled up the sleeves and wasn't sorry to be covered to her ankles. The intimacy she had naively sought suddenly struck her as having come at too high a price and she was more self-conscious in the aftermath than she had been beforehand.

'I thought you'd be hungry,' Leo remarked with a casual movement of his hand pointing out the catering trolley that had appeared. 'I don't know what you like so I ordered a selection.'

'You have someone in a kitchen cooking for you at *four* in the morning?' Grace exclaimed in astonishment while being grateful for the distraction provided by the food. Wandering barefoot over to the trolley, she lifted the covers to inspect the mouth-watering options on offer. Her tummy gave a hungry growl, hopefully concealed by the clatter of the coffee jug lid she lifted and dropped again. In silence she helped herself to coffee and a plate of elaborate supper bites.

It was ironic though that since meeting Leo she had never been more aware of his compelling presence than she was in that charged silence. He had changed into jeans and a blue T-shirt, his black hair tousled, shiny and damp from the shower, his lean, darkly handsome face shadowed by dark stubble. Apprehensive though she was about the risk of consequences, she had to admit that Leo still looked amazing and the epitome of every fantasy she had ever had about a man.

'I have a doctor on call, if you want—'

'No.' Grace leapt straight in before he could say it because the morning-after treatment that could stop a pregnancy developing was not a choice she was willing to make. Even though a

pregnancy would damage her chances of qualifying in medicine. 'That's not an option for me.'

'I had to make the option available,' Leo murmured without any perceptible reaction. 'When are you flying home?'

'The day after tomorrow.' Grace sat down in an opulent armchair.

'I will want your address and phone number. This is not a situation I would treat lightly.' Leo served himself with coffee, betraying all the awkwardness of a male who wasn't used to waiting on himself and who had rather expected his companion to take on the role of hostess.

Grace allowed herself to look at Leo for only the second time since she had left the bathroom. Whether she liked it or not, he had gone up in her estimation.

'If you give me your contact details, we won't need to discuss this any further. I only need to add the assurance that if there is any…er…development, I will provide you with my full support.'

'Yes.' Grace almost shrugged because she

knew words were cheap. Leo was saying the right things but only he and his conscience could know how reliable he would be in such trying circumstances as those of an unplanned pregnancy. After all, her own father had talked her mother out of the termination she had decided on when she had fallen pregnant as a student. Grace's father had promised her mother that he would marry her and help her raise their child and then he had run off with another woman and left Keira Donovan literally holding the baby. That had been in the days when being an unmarried mother had still been a real stigma and a source of family shame.

Leo settled a notepad and pen down on the table beside Grace. She printed her address and phone number and returned the pad to the table. As she did so, she yawned. 'I'm sorry, I'm very sleepy…'

'It's late…go to bed,' he murmured quietly.

Grace thought of the hassle of arriving back at the marina before dawn, finding her way back to the apartment block and then sitting in Reception until Stuart took his leave. 'I'll stay…at least you have a bed.'

'A bed?' Leo queried, recognising her exhaustion in her pale face and heavy eyes.

Grace climbed into the bed still clad in the robe.

'I wasn't going to touch you again,' Leo remarked drily.

'Obviously I've offended your ego and I'm sorry,' Grace mumbled.

As she closed her eyes Leo peeled off his own clothing, although he retained his boxers and slid into the other side of the bed, dousing the lights. 'What did you mean about having a bed?'

'Our apartment is only one bedroom and my cousin met a man the first day,' she whispered. 'I've been sitting up in Reception most nights so that she can be with him—'

'That's outrageous!' Leo cut in.

'No, it's not. Jenna's family paid for her to go on holiday with her best friend.' Briefly she explained. 'Now that she's met Stuart, I'm surplus to requirements.'

'Surely her parents would be furious if they knew how she was treating you?'

'What Jenna wants, Jenna gets,' Grace muttered drowsily, her voice trailing down in volume. 'It's always been that way. She's the daughter, the little princess…I'm the niece they took in out of the kindness of their heart.'

'But to make such distinctions between two children in the same family!' Leo began angrily until it dawned on him that Grace had fallen asleep.

A moment later, the echo of his own words still ringing in his ears, he realised that there were remarkable similarities between Grace's situation with her cousin and his own non-relationship with the half-brother he hated. Yes, in his home too, the *same* distinction had been made in favour of the legitimate firstborn son, Leo. For the first time Leo was recognising an angle that he had never even considered before: Bastien's side of the story. Was it really so surprising that Bastien had always seemed to seethe with resentment as a child and had matured into a fiercely competitive and aggressive male? He was sobered by the unfamiliar thoughts afflicting him, and it was a long time before Leo fell asleep.

CHAPTER FOUR

'NO, PLEASE DON'T tell me it's been great!' Grace urged Leo with a rueful laugh as, ever gracious, he saw her into the speedboat that would whisk her back to the *real* world, rather than the fantasy in which she had ordered her own personal perfect breakfast directly from Leo's personal chef.

'Why not?' Leo demanded, strangely unsettled by her apparent good humour at leaving him.

'Because you *know* it's been a disaster for you from start to finish but you're too polite to say it. I was absolutely not what you expected,' Grace pointed out bluntly, taking a seat in the launch.

Leo, rarely put out of countenance, felt heat sear his cheekbones and thought that she really was extraordinarily unusual for her sex, when she said exactly what she thought and felt without chagrin, revealing not an iota of the vanity he had believed that every woman possessed. 'I will be in touch—'

'Not necessary,' Grace cut in briskly as if he were a five-year-old importuning a busy teacher.

His strong jaw line clenched. '*I* will decide what's necessary,' Leo delivered, losing patience.

From the upper deck, Leo watched the launch convey Grace back to the marina. He was assailed by a vague sense of something unfinished…of regret? His jaw set hard as granite. He had almost asked her to stay with him until it was time for her to fly home. *Why?* She had spoken the truth, after all: it *had* been a disaster. Instead of an experienced woman and a sexual marathon he had landed a virgin and then there had been the mishap with the condom. His teeth gritted together. When he had registered that for some inexplicable reason he was in no hurry to see Grace leave, his blood had run cold on the suspicion that he was feeling more than he was willing to feel for any woman, and from that point on he had been keen to see her depart. Yet the sound of her sobbing his name in orgasm still echoed in his ears and his body hardened as he remembered all too well the tight, hot feel of hers. From his point of view, although there had been too little of it, the sex had been stellar. In fact there had been something oddly, dangerously addictive about Grace Donovan and getting rid of her fast had been absolutely the right action to take!

Three weeks after that day, Grace did a pregnancy test in the bathroom of her aunt and uncle's home.

Her nerves were shot to hell and her mood had been on a steady downward slope for days when her menstrual cycle had failed to kick in on the expected date. Unfortunately pregnancy tests were very expensive and Grace had forced herself to wait until there was little risk of the test providing her with a potentially false result that would require yet another test to be done. And now she was bracing herself for the moment of truth even while her training had already provided her with good reason to be afraid. The very last thing she had required earlier that week was a blatantly impatient text from Leo Zikos asking for news that she did not yet have, so she had simply ignored it.

Her breath hissed in her dry throat when she studied the result: positive. Hell roast the wretched man, she thought ridiculously, why couldn't he have been sterile? Instead they were both young and healthy and the odds had not been in their favour. *Pregnant!* Fear and no small amount of horror made Grace break out in a cold sweat because nobody knew better than her how very hard, if not impossible, it would be for her to complete her medical studies with a child in tow and no supportive partner. Suddenly she was furious with herself for not having protected her own body better simply because she had failed to foresee the need. She had assumed that she would always be in total control and Leo Zikos with his stunning dark eyes had shown her different. But at what cost?

Leo…stray thoughts and recollections of Leo

had littered the past weeks while Grace had struggled to put the entire episode behind her and continue as normal. She had discovered that she had a softer, dreamier side to her character that she had never suspected. Well, so much for that, she thought cynically, stuffing the pregnancy-test paraphernalia back into the plastic bag to be discreetly dumped. Would she tell Leo? Undoubtedly she would tell him…*eventually* but not until she had decided what to do. Right at that minute she had more to worry about than taking time out to contact a male who had nothing other than money to offer her in terms of support. She suspected that Leo would expect her to have a termination and when she refused to give him a 'tidy' conclusion to the development he would be furious and resentful of her decision.

Would he be the exact opposite of the father she had never met? Grace wrinkled her nose, not wanting to think along those lines. She was too intelligent not to be aware that her mother had fed her daughter a steady diet of her own martyred bitterness. Sadly, Grace had been too young to be told such things, too innocent to be anything other than deeply hurt by an absent father who had never felt the need to look for his eldest child. Her father had other children now; she knew after finding him on Facebook that she had half-siblings with the same red hair, the children of the woman he had married after deserting her mother. Yet her father had pleaded for Grace to be given the chance of life before she was even born and how could she do any less for her own baby?

Grace adored babies, but she had believed that the opportunity to have children lay far, far away in her future. And now that everything had changed she was struggling not to think in either personal or sentimental terms about the baby. After all, after her own chequered experience as a child she knew that the best possible option for her baby would be an adoption by two parents with a stable home and everything Grace herself was currently unable to provide.

Didn't she owe her child the very best possible start in life? What on earth could she give in comparison? Her own mother had frankly struggled to cope with the weighty responsibilities of being a single parent. Keira Donovan had often resented her daughter, blaming her for the loss of her youthful freedom. There had always been a shortage of money for necessities and Grace had often been left in the care of unsuitable babysitters. Most telling of all, Grace was painfully aware of how much she herself had longed to have a stable father figure when she was a child. She was terrified of failing her own child the way her mother had failed her. But while her brain reminded her of all those distressingly practical facts, a more visceral response to motherhood deep down inside her was agonised by the concept of handing her baby over to someone else to raise.

The locked door rattled. 'Grace? Are you in there?' It was her aunt's voice, sharp and demanding.

Lifting the bag, Grace unlocked the door and prepared to step past the older woman.

Instead Della Donovan laid her hand on Grace's arm to prevent her from walking away. 'Are you pregnant?' she demanded thinly.

Bemused by the question when she had not shared her concern with anyone, Grace stiffened, her brows lifting in a startled arc. 'Why are you asking me that?'

'Oh, that could be my fault.' Jenna sighed with mock sympathy, pausing at the top of the stairs. 'I was behind you in the checkout at the supermarket and I couldn't help noticing the test…'

Grace lost colour. 'Yes, I'm pregnant,' she admitted stonily.

Her aunt, always a volatile woman, immediately lost her temper. By the time she had finished shouting, threatening and verbally abusing her niece for her morals, Grace knew where she stood and that she could no longer remain in her aunt and uncle's home. Della had said things about Grace and her late mother that Grace knew that she would never forget. White as paper and numb with shock in the aftermath of that upsetting confrontation, she went into her room, phoned Matt and pulled out her suitcase; there was nothing else she could do. Her life, the life she had worked so hard to achieve, was falling apart even faster than she had feared, she acknowledged with a sinking heart.

At the outset of that same week, Leo had texted Grace but she hadn't replied and he was tired of waiting and waking up in the middle of the night *wondering…*

In little more than two months' time he was getting married and Marina had made him more than aware of that fact by calling him to ask his opinion on various questions of bridal trivia that he couldn't have cared less about. Nothing more important had entered those conversations and it had convinced him that he was the only one of them with doubts.

Sadly, even the smallest doubt had not featured in Leo's original blueprint for his future. He fixed on a goal, made decisions, brought plans to fruition and that was that. He didn't do wondering about *what if*! He understood perfectly why he had ended up with Grace Donovan that night. He had been angry with Marina and full of misgivings about what their future together might hold. Regrettably, however, that still did not explain why Grace had hit him like a torpedo striking his yacht below the waterline. It did not explain why she had given him the most incredible sexual experience of his far from innocent life to date or why given the smallest excuse he would have repeated that night.

Consequently, he had checked out who Grace Donovan was while he waited to hear from her and what he had learned from that comprehensive investigation had only made him more confused. Her early childhood had been appalling and her adolescence not much kinder. It was a credit to her strength of character that she had achieved so much, regardless of those disadvantages. Yet there was still so much he didn't understand. Why would a young woman as well-informed as a fifth-year medical student not take extra contraceptive precautions? And why had she avoided telling him what she was studying? He had also taken on board the reality that an unplanned pregnancy would probably wreak greater havoc on her life than it would on his.

When the curiosity, the unanswered questions and the need to know whether or not they had a problem rose to a critical level, Leo refused to wait to hear from Grace any longer. He gave his driver her address and compressed his lips, annoyed that Grace was forcing him to confront her. How *could* he walk away and hope for the best? How could he possibly risk marrying Marina without knowing for sure? The answer to both questions was that Leo could not ignore the situation, being all too well aware of the likely repercussions should Grace prove to be pregnant. On a deeper level, however, Leo could simply not believe that his legendary good fortune with women would crash and burn over something as basic as a sperm and an egg meeting in the wrong womb.

An hour later, Leo was considerably less naïve,

having struck a blank at Grace's former address. The frigid blonde in her forties who accepted his business card changed her attitude a little once she noticed his limousine and became more helpful but Leo still couldn't get away fast enough. He really wanted nothing to do with a woman who had thrown out the mother of *his* future child—a phrase with a shocking depth he could not quite digest at that moment—like some pantomime little match girl and who had earlier in the dialogue referred witheringly to Grace in unjust terms that had implied she was some high-living veteran slut.

Thee mou, he was going to be a father… whether he liked it or not. Leo breathed in slow and deep, traumatised by the concept, and rang Marina straight away.

'Oh, dear,' Marina sighed with what he rather suspected was bogus sympathy. 'That rather tops my misbehaviour with my married man, doesn't it? What do you want to do?'

'We'll meet up and talk.'

'No, I suspect that right now you need to be

doing that with the baby's mother, *not* with me,' Marina remarked heavily. 'What a ghastly mess, Leo!'

Leo ground his teeth together but there was nothing he could say in his own defence. He felt as though his smooth, perfectly organised life had been violently derailed without warning. Were all his carefully laid plans about his future domestic life to come to nothing now because his contraception had let him down? he questioned bitterly. He swore under his breath and gave the driver the second address he had acquired while wondering exactly who Matt Davison was and what his connection was to Grace. It was not that he was possessive, of course, it was solely the unpleasant awareness that Grace Donovan was very probably going to be the mother of his first child and the nature of her character mattered much more now than it had the night they had met.

Was he already travelling down the destructive path his father had trodden before him? His bitterness hardened. No, he was not going to marry one woman for her wealth while another, poorer one carried his child and thankfully love didn't enter the picture in any way. Anatole Zikos had married Leo's mother while loving his mistress and had never conquered that craving. Leo prided himself on being infinitely more down-to-earth and less emotional than his father. While his situation with Grace might be starting out as a mess, he would swiftly organise the threatening chaos into something more acceptable that both he *and* Grace could live with.

Grace was humming under her breath while she cooked supper, grateful that the smell of the chicken and vegetables didn't stir up nausea the way the scent of anything fried seemed to do. At least her studies hadn't started yet. She was at the start of a reading week, set aside for home study.

The doorbell went and she wondered if Matt had forgotten his key. Her friend's parents had died when he was eighteen, leaving him with the means to buy his own apartment. She was comfortable living in Matt's guest room but, concerned that she was taking advantage of his good nature, she had taken over the cooking and the cleaning to demonstrate her appreciation of his hospitality.

Barefoot, she padded out to the hall, a slim, casually clad figure in skinny jeans and a striped navy and white sweater, her vibrant long hair restrained in a braid that hung halfway down her back.

'Leo…' she pronounced numbly, shattered to find the leading character in her daydreams in the flesh on the doorstep.

'Why didn't you answer my text?'

'I'm afraid I didn't have an answer for you at the time.'

Leo was so close to Grace that he could tell she was wearing no make-up and the sheer glow of her creamy cheeks and bright pale green eyes knocked him flat. She was even more beautiful than he remembered and a fleeting memory of her pale hands stroking down over his stomach gripped him, resulting in a stirringly strong surge of lust that he very much could have done without.

'Your aunt threw you out.'

'So, that's how you found out where I was living! My uncle came to see me the day before yesterday. He asked me to come home with him but I don't want to cause trouble between them, so I can't,' Grace admitted, distinctly overpowered by Leo's proximity because she wasn't wearing heels and without them Leo towered over her, all broad shoulders and long powerful legs, arrogant dark head tipped back to gaze down at her. And looking up at that moment seemed a definite mistake because his brilliant dark golden eyes were framed by black curling lashes as long and striking as any she had ever seen on a man. He had absolutely gorgeous eyes that froze her to the spot and made her stare while her heart rate accelerated, her mouth ran dry and a knot of undeniable excitement tightened and then unfurled in her chest.

It's just attraction, you dummy, she scolded herself a split second later, her skin already cooling with dismay at the strength of her reaction to him. But Leo Zikos was an extraordinarily handsome man and it was hardly surprising that she was reacting to that reality, particularly when she had already slept with him and knew that below his business suit he was even more incredibly fanciable and impressive than he was clothed. That last inappropriate thought struck Grace with such effect and so much embarrassment and self-loathing that her pale skin flamed scarlet, mortified heat crawling over her entire skin surface.

'I've never seen anyone blush that deeply,' Leo confided in wonderment, watching the flush trail down her long white throat and dapple that fine skin with a warmer colour.

'You're supposed to pretend you didn't notice, not embarrass me about it further,' Grace told him roundly. 'I used to go through agonies blushing when I was a kid. It's the fault of my fair skin—it's very conspicuous.'

Leo didn't know where the conversation had gone, but then he hadn't come with a prepared script, and as she strolled back into the kitchen to tend a steaming wok a key sounded in the front door and someone else arrived. Leo wheeled round to inspect a fresh-faced young man in his twenties with brown hair and bright blue eyes behind earnest spectacles.

'Matt…meet Leo,' Grace said quietly.

'Oh, right…er…' The hapless Matt managed to smile at Grace and then deal Leo a very different look of angry disapproval. 'Of course, you'll want to talk. Take him to the living room. I'll take charge of whatever you're cooking.'

'Thanks, Matt,' Grace said comfortably, pressing open a door off the hall and waving a guiding hand in Leo's direction.

Leo's talent had always been reading other people and he clearly saw Matt's suppressed hostility and Grace's complete unawareness of it and probably of its most likely source.

'What's Matt to you?' Leo asked the instant Grace closed the door.

'A good friend…and thank goodness for him. At such short notice the university couldn't find me decent accommodation anywhere but a hostel, so I was grateful for Matt's invite,' Grace proffered truthfully. 'Matt and I are on the same course.'

'Why did your family throw you out?' Leo enquired baldly, stationing himself by the window of the small room, which was cluttered with books, many of them lying half-open.

Grace gave him a wry glance. 'I think you already know why.'

'But that news should have come from you directly to me,' Leo told her grimly. 'I had a right to know first!'

'And perhaps you would've done were we in a relationship,' Grace countered quietly. 'But since we're not, the situation is rather different.'

Even greater tension filled Leo, stiffening the muscles in his broad shoulders, his clean-cut strong jawline hardening at her stubborn reminder of facts he considered to be more destructive than helpful. 'If you're pregnant, we definitely *have* a relationship,' he contradicted.

Grace wrinkled her nose. 'Well, I am having

your baby,' she conceded reluctantly. 'But we don't have to have *any* kind of a relationship!'

'And how do you work that out?' Leo gritted, becoming steadily more annoyed by her dismissive attitude.

'I can manage fine on my own. I'm very independent,' Grace informed him. 'I'll continue with my studies, hopefully have the baby during the Easter term break and give it up for adoption.'

'Adoption?' Leo was thoroughly disconcerted and stunned by her solution, that being a possibility he hadn't even considered. 'You're planning to have our child adopted?'

Grace pleated her slender fingers together to conceal the fact that her hands were trembling while she battled to tamp down her distress. 'I know it won't be an easy decision to make when the time comes, Leo. I don't want to give my child up but I was brought up by a single parent until I was nine years old and my mother really did struggle to meet the demands of that role.'

'But—' Leo clamped his lips shut on an in-

stinctive protest while he fought to master emotions he had never felt before. Of course her reference to adoption had taken him very much by surprise. Even so, the very thought of never knowing his own child and not even having the right to see him or her genuinely appalled Leo. Even his own instinctive rejection of her proposition was a revelation that shocked him. 'I don't think I could approve that option.'

'As far as I know you don't legally have any say in the matter,' Grace retorted in an apologetic rather than challenging tone. 'Only married fathers have those kinds of rights.'

'Then I'll marry you.'

Grace groaned at that knee-jerk reaction. 'Don't be silly, Leo. Strangers don't get married.'

Leo lifted his dark head high and surveyed her with glittering golden eyes that were mesmeric in their intensity. 'I don't care how we go about it but while you may not want our child, I *do* and I am prepared to raise that child, should that become necessary.'

It was Grace's turn to be thrown off balance

and she paled. 'When it comes to my preferences, it's not a matter of my wanting or *not* wanting the baby…it's much more a matter of what *I* can offer my child and how best *I* could meet my child's needs. And the truth is that as a student with no home of my own or current earning power, I've got very little to offer.'

'While I on the other hand have a great deal to offer and could help you in any way necessary,' Leo cut in succinctly. 'And in the short term I think it would be best if you came to live in my London apartment.'

'*Your* apartment?' Grace echoed in disbelief. 'Why on earth would I move into your apartment?'

'Because that's *my* baby you're carrying and I intend to be fully involved in giving you whatever support you need until our child is born,' Leo declared without hesitation.

'I'm perfectly comfortable here with Matt.' Grace groaned, her brow tightening with stress because Leo was saying things and offering options she had not anticipated and she had already spent several days anxiously worrying over her alternatives before coming to the conclusion that adoption was the most sensible answer to all her concerns. Now Leo was demanding a share of that responsibility and complicating the situation with his own ideas.

'Staying here with Matt is unwise,' Leo murmured drily.

'In what way? He's a very good friend.'

'But that's not all he wants to be,' Leo incised. 'Matt is in love with you.'

Grace was aghast. 'That's complete nonsense!'

'A friend would be relieved when the father of your child arrived to take an interest in your predicament. But a would-be lover feels threatened and annoyed and that's what he is,' Leo spelled out impatiently. 'You're not stupid, Grace. Your very good friend wants you living here with him because he's in love with you.'

'That's completely untrue.' Strikingly taken aback by his contention, Grace turned away in an uncoordinated half-circle. She was picturing Matt, his behaviour and his caring ways while wondering if it was possible that she could have been so blind that she had not noticed the depth of his feelings for her. 'What would you know about it anyway?'

'I only know what I saw in his face once he realised who I was,' Leo said grimly. 'You're really not doing him any favours staying on here... unless of course you're planning on returning his feelings?'

'Er...that would be a no,' Grace muttered guiltily while recognising the terrible unwelcome truth in Leo's arguments. If it was true that Matt wanted more than friendship from her, it was equally true that there was no prospect of her offering it. The intensity of her attraction to Leo had concluded for ever any prospect of her trying to make more of her relationship with Matt. From the instant Leo had taught her of her own capacity to feel so much more mentally and physically than she had ever dreamt she could feel, her former conviction that she and Matt would make a great couple had died.

'Then move into my apartment where you will not be under pressure,' Leo advised softly.

Grace wanted to slap Leo for cutting through all her possible protests by employing the one credible argument calculated to make her think again. Matt spent a lot of time with her. Matt was always there for her, eternally helping her and discussing her worries, but she was doing Matt a disservice by living with him if he was hoping for more than friendship from her. In that scenario the sooner she got out of Matt's home and put some distance between them, the better, she reasoned guiltily.

'When?'

'I see no point in wasting time. Why not now? You can't have that much stuff to pack. You've only been here a couple of days,' he pointed out smoothly, reining back any hint of satisfaction in his demeanour.

Matt was threatening to get involved in a situation that was none of his business and Leo wanted him eliminated before he interfered and caused trouble.

Waiting in the small reception room, he listened to Matt raise his voice and Grace mute hers as she explained that she was moving out. The mother of his child, historically not a happy role in his family experience, but if adoption was in the offing he needed to come up with a viable alternative. Grace hadn't even paused to consider the idea when he'd suggested marrying her. Cynical amusement filled Leo because he was too clever to cherish illusions about what made him so appealing to the female sex in general: first and foremost his great wealth followed by his looks and his sexual prowess. Yet Grace had thumbed her nose at that winning combination, doing what no other woman had done before in rejecting him. Although she had not rejected him the night when it all began, Leo savoured with an appreciation that was yet to pall in spite of the news he had received earlier.

A battered suitcase, two boxes of files and a pile of books now littered the hall. Matt insisted on helping them transport Grace's possessions out to the waiting limousine and Leo's driver climbed out in consternation to whisk the case out of his employer's grip while two of his body-guards grabbed up the boxes.

'Look after her…don't hurt her,' Matt breathed in a charged and warning undertone before Leo could climb into his limousine.

'I won't,' Leo countered, his accented drawl curt and cool, his ego challenged by the tone of that advice.

'I can't believe I'm doing this,' Grace lamented, because she was already suffering second thoughts. Leo had extracted her from Matt's flat at the speed of light.

'Right now, you need time out to decide what you want to do next,' Leo told her levelly. 'A few days…a few weeks, whatever it takes. You shouldn't be trying to make life-changing decisions virtually overnight.'

'You don't want me to go for adoption?' Grace said, her slim frame tensing, her fingers folding together tightly on her lap.

'Adoption entails you cutting me out of the situation entirely. *Why* would you want to do that?' Leo queried softly. 'I am willing to help in every way possible. There are other options and I think you should consider them.'

Grace breathed in slow and deep, fighting the sense that he was putting her on the spot because she knew that was unjust. She was in a highly stressful situation and any decision she made would put her under pressure. 'This year of my degree I have to spend a lot of time working long unsocial hours in hospitals. Coping with that while pregnant will be a challenge.'

'We can find some way to work around the problems. I've made an appointment for you with a doctor, who's a friend of mine,' Leo told her quietly. 'We're calling in with him first—'

'A doctor? Why, for goodness' sake?' Grace demanded impatiently.

'I want confirmation of your pregnancy and the reassurance that you are in good health,' he admitted quietly.

Grace breathed in deep, suppressing her frustration. He had a right to that official endorsement, she reasoned ruefully.

Leo's friend was in private practice and her pregnancy test was processed at supersonic speed before the suave, smoothly spoken doctor gave her a brief physical check-up and the usual advice offered to pregnant women.

Having satisfied Leo's request, Grace was quiet when she slid back into his limousine and thinking about her baby. Possibly she had been a little too quick to consider the avenue of adoption, a solution that would enable her to continue her life after the birth as though she had never been pregnant. Obviously the idea of reclaiming normality had appeal but what sort of normality would it be when she had to live for ever after with the awareness that she had given up her baby? A cold chill clenched Grace's spine at the prospect of that ultimate consequence. Adoption was final and could well sentence her to live with a secret heartbreak and sense of loss for the rest of her days. Suddenly, the chance to think at her leisure, while not having to worry about where or how she lived or what other people thought, shone like the most luxurious indulgence in front of her. Leo, she dimly appreciated, could talk a lot of good sense when it suited him to do so.

When they arrived at the block of exclusive apartments where Leo lived, his guards and her luggage went in the service lift, imprisoning her with Leo in the opulent confines of a far smaller and less utilitarian lift. She met his stunning eyes once and her heart stuttered as she immediately turned her head away, only to be greeted with a mirrored reflection of him instead: the luxuriant blue-black hair she wanted to tousle with her fingers, the arrogant angle of his head and the firm jut of his jaw, the sheer blazing confidence that inexplicably drew her like a magnet. Her mouth drying, she swallowed with difficulty. She felt out of step with herself, challenged to recognise the stranger she became in Leo's presence, a stranger with random, often inappropriate thoughts and no control over her own body.

'Stop fighting it,' Leo growled soft and low, his abrasive accent purring along the syllables.

Grace glanced up. 'Fighting what?'

'This...'

And he reached for her, pulling her up against his big powerful frame with easy strength. In unmistakeable contact with the long, hard length of his erection Grace's tummy flipped and her knees turned to water. Dangerous heat shimmied between her legs.

'It's crazy—'

'The most powerful craving I've ever felt,' Leo sliced in. 'I felt it the first time I saw you. I fought it to let you walk away. But I'm done being sensible.'

Completely disconcerted by that blunt admission, Grace parted dry lips. *'But—'*

'No...buts, *meli mou*,' Leo husked against her cheek, his breath fanning her parted lips. 'The words you're looking for are *Yes, Leo*.'

A strangled little sound of amusement escaped Grace. 'I hope you're the patient type?'

'Not even remotely.' Strong arms banding round her, Leo lifted her up against him and claimed her mouth with a voracious driving passion that curled her toes and made her nails dig into his shoulder. When she made a half-hearted attempt to evade him his arms merely clamped tighter round her while he delved deeper into her mouth to send a current of fire arrowing through her quivering length. He tasted spicy and sweet and so unbelievably good she couldn't get enough of him. She was barely aware of the lift doors whirring open or of the momentary separation of their mouths as he cannoned into a doorway with a muffled Greek expletive. Indeed the entire experience was like a time out from her brain because a hunger she couldn't fight had taken control.

CHAPTER FIVE

LEO LAID HER down on a wide bed. 'I want you to know that I didn't bring you here for this,' he breathed rawly. 'I didn't plan it.'

His lean, darkly handsome features were taut with hungry frustration and the strangest hint of vulnerability, and for a split second Grace almost raised her fingers to trace the compressed line of his lips. Instead she got a grip of herself and let her hand fall back from his shoulder to lie by her side. Her body was singing a very different message, all revved up like a racing car at the starting line. She was startlingly aware of every erogenous zone she possessed and his pronounced effect on her. Her breasts felt swollen while a hollow ache throbbed at the very centre of her. It was sexual need, plain sexual need, she repeated carefully to herself, as if by acknowledging that she could minimise the effects and suppress them.

'I intended for us to sit down over a civilised dinner and talk,' Leo grated impatiently, stepping back from the bed as if he didn't trust himself that close to her. 'But I can't keep my hands off you!'

He made Grace feel totally irresistible and she marvelled at the sensation and the new buoyancy it gave to her sadly depleted ego, battered by her aunt's abuse, her cousin's scorn and Matt's heartfelt and apologetic, 'How could you be so stupid?' There Leo stood, breathtakingly beautiful, rich and charismatic and he still wanted her when she was sure he had to have many more lovely and laid-back female options.

'I think it cuts both ways,' she admitted not quite steadily, just looking at him and wanting him so much it almost hurt while telling herself that was entirely and unforgivably superficial.

Leo came down on one knee on the edge of the bed. 'You...*think*?'

'Know,' she conceded breathlessly, stinging

arousal assailing her nipples as she collided with his spectacular dark golden eyes. She thought she would die if he didn't touch her, told herself that she deserved to die if she let him, but she couldn't lie about the overwhelming surge of hunger that lit her up like a firework.

'I want you so much it's driving me insane,' Leo husked, coming down to her in one driven movement to seal her to the mattress with his weight. 'I don't like the feeling that I'm not in control...'

Grace didn't like it either and was taken aback that they could be so similar in outlook. Her fingers lifted involuntarily and laced through the blue-black hair falling across his brow. Rain lashed the window across the room and a smouldering silence fell indoors. Her heart was racing and against her breast she could feel the quickened thump of his. Dense black lashes lifted on his stunning eyes and she forgot to breathe, registering that somewhere along the way, and without ever pausing to think it through, she had begun developing feelings for Leos Zikos that went way beyond what she had once envisaged.

For a split second fear grabbed her, fear of being hurt, humiliated and rejected, but she pushed the reactions away and buried them deep. Just for a few hours, she promised herself, she would live only for the moment in a little safe pool of non-judgemental peace because soon enough she would be forced to deal with the consequences of her accidental pregnancy.

Leo smoothed a stray strand of red hair behind her ear, noting how small her ear was and that at their last encounter he had miscounted the freckles on her nose. There were five, not four, tiny brown speckles that only accentuated the clarity of her luminous porcelain skin. He sank his hands beneath her, lifting her up to peel off her sweater. She was pregnant, he reminded himself in a daze, for that awareness was still so new to him that it felt unreal. He would have to be careful and that would be a challenge when his raw need for her was threatening to explode out of restraint.

'Is it all right for us to do this?' he murmured a tad awkwardly.

'Good grief, Leo, I'm as healthy as a cart-horse!' Grace countered, reddening hotly as his appreciative gaze dropped down to the bountiful swell of her breasts in a lace-cupped bra.

'But infinitely more beautiful and sensual,' Leo purred, fighting an impractical urge to stay welded to her and finally sliding off the bed to strip off his suit. 'So delicate...and yet voluptuous.'

A reluctant grin slanted Grace's mouth. 'You really do have the gift of the gab, as my Irish mother used to say. Women must drop like nine-pins around you in receipt of all that flattery.'

In Leo's experience women were infinitely more aggressive in their desire to catch his eye and share his bed. His sculpted mouth quirked at her innocence. He dropped his shirt on the floor, ropes of abdominal muscle flexing across his torso below her admiring gaze. Grace dragged her attention from him in embarrassment and shimmied out of her jeans, blushing at the schoolgirl knickers she sported beneath. She had never had the money to buy prettier underwear. That random thought took her brain off the disturbing truth that she was succumbing to Leo's magnetism all over again. Was that wrong?

She wanted him; she wanted him every bit as much as he seemed to want her. He was the father of the baby she carried and he was neither irresponsible nor uncaring and there was absolutely no reason why they should not be together again…was there? Did she have to be sensible Grace all the time? She recalled the end result of rebelling against her sensible self the night she had met Leo. But then that axe had already fallen, she reminded herself doggedly, quickly talking herself into staying exactly where she was.

'You've got that thinking-too-hard look on your face again,' Leo chided, pulling her into his arms. 'It makes you look incredibly serious.'

His body was so hot against the faintly chilled coolness of her own, so hot in temperature and so deliciously different. He was rough where she was smooth, hard where she was soft. Desire snaked through her like a sharp-cutting knife, clenching low down in her pelvis. Her fingertips grazed across his muscular torso as he leant over her. The kiss he stole was explosive. He sucked and nibbled at her lower lip, all teasing and sex, stirring her up with the occasional plunge of his tongue.

Grace scored her fingers down a powerful hair-roughened thigh and circled his throbbing hardness before pushing him back against the pillows with her free hand. Startled, Leo began to raise his shoulders off the pillows while Grace zeroed in on her objective. Her soft sultry mouth closed over him like a glove and any resistance he had faded fast. Dangling strands of red hair danced across his skin with her every movement.

'OK?' she said, looking up at him, her face as red as a ripe apple.

'Better than…way better,' Leo admitted unevenly, mesmerised by the way she was touching him, craving it more with every passing second.

As she took him deep, his hand tangled in her tumbled hair and excitement filled her as he arched his hips up to her for more. A low groan sounded in his throat, an almost animalistic purr, while her fingers toyed with him and her tongue glided over him. Her pace quickened, her mouth moving over him faster and faster.

'Bloody spectacular...' Leo grated between clenched teeth as she took him up and over in the longest, hottest release of his life.

Grace lay back, feeling vindicated, feeling empowered, no longer the shy, ignorant virgin in need of guidance or instruction. He had really enjoyed that and she knew it. Leo turned her flushed face towards him, dark eyes still tawny gold with arousal. 'You always surprise me.'

Her bra came adrift, his hands kneading her aching flesh while his thumbs skimmed her distended nipples. She closed her eyes, losing herself in a world of sensation while he licked his way down over her body, tugging her knickers out of his path to discover the warm, wet welcome already awaiting him because nothing had ever quite excited Grace as much as her view of Leo shedding his smooth sophistication and crying out from the pleasure she was giving him.

With a hungry growl he eased over her, his recovery rate exceeding her expectations when the heated probe of his engorged shaft pushed against her most tender flesh. A surge of excitement made her inner muscles clench tightly round him. Her heart was hammering. She wanted this, she wanted *him* so much she was trembling and breathless, on a high of such joyful anticipation she could hardly contain it.

'You feel amazing,' Leo rasped, struggling for control as he worked his way gently into the depths of her glorious body when he didn't feel remotely gentle.

Grace tilted up her hips and locked her slim legs round him in acceptance. 'I'm not made of eggshell,' she whispered teasingly.

With a groan of relief, Leo surrendered to the raw need riding him, easing out of her tight channel to slam back in again with a glorious sense of satisfaction.

Grace couldn't catch her breath as he moved with animalistic power, powering into her with a hard driven sensuality that filled her with splintering excitement. Her whole body was reaching for and craving the ultimate crest and when it reached it she soared high as heaven. The intense pleasure radiated through her in an astonishing crescendo of sensation that left her trembling with little aftershocks of delight for several minutes afterwards.

On another level, she was conscious of Leo leaving the bed, doubtless to dispose of the contraception he had employed. She waited for him to return and then heard the shower running, slowly and unhappily realising that there would be no cosy togetherness in the aftermath of intimacy. That surprised her, for Leo was very prone to affectionate touching, not stand-offish in any way. Was he afraid of giving her the wrong message? Apprehensive that a little cuddle might make her assume that he felt more for her than he actually did?

Grace shifted uneasily in the bed, her brain

now clear of the overwhelming pleasure that had left her mindless. She was painfully aware that she was developing feelings for Leo Zikos, far beyond the boundaries of those she had first envisaged. Considering how insanely attractive Leo was, she supposed her reaction to him was fairly normal and naturally there was something even more attractive about his insatiable desire for her ordinary self, never mind the fact that he was the father of her baby. Obviously she didn't want to get hurt by falling for someone who didn't feel the same way. But then, nobody wanted to get their heart broken and this was not only a time for her to consider her future as a mother, but also a time in which they could get to know each other better and explore their feelings.

By the time Leo came back to bed, Grace was sound asleep. Around dawn she shifted up against Leo and the sheer novelty value of being in bed with another person was probably what awakened him. In the darkness, he lay still, listening to Grace's even breathing. He frowned and very gently removed the arm he had inexplicably draped round Grace before quietly easing out of the bed to pull on jeans and a shirt. He padded through to the vast expanse of the main reception room and checked his phone for messages.

There was a text from his father: Anatole would be in London on Saturday and wanted to know if Leo would still be around. Leo almost groaned out loud. He would be on the other side of the world by then but he now needed to move Grace to another location because the London apartment was used by both his father and his brother. Leaving Grace in residence would entail explanations that Leo was not yet ready to make.

He raked impatient fingers through his tousled black hair. What was he playing at? What the hell had he been playing at when he took Grace back to bed again? That was no answer to the mess they were both in and had probably only complicated everything more. He was maddened by his sudden unprecedented loss of restraint and discipline the night before and exasperated by what he saw as his own irrational behaviour.

Sex had always been a purely physical exercise for Leo. Anything even one step beyond simple sex was dangerous in his view because it could open him up to the risk of destructive attachments and desires. He had not had to worry about that before because he had never connected in any more lasting way with a woman he had been intimate with.

He swore under his breath, grasping that it was a little late in the day to acknowledge that he was getting in too deep with Grace Donovan. Hadn't they enough of a connection in the child she had conceived? Getting involved in an affair with Grace would be foolish because when it finished relations would inevitably sour between them and potentially damage his future relationship with his child. Why hadn't he thought about that reality? Why hadn't he thought about what he would be encouraging if he had sex with her again? Most probably raising expectations he was highly unlikely to fulfil?

As Leo poured himself a whiskey from a crystal decanter it seemed to him that his libido had been doing all his thinking for him. That shook him inside out. In fact he broke out in a cold sweat at that knowledge while he paced the pale limestone floor. He drained his glass and set it down with a definitive snap. Was he more like his father than he had ever suspected? Too weak and selfish to behave honourably? More likely than most men to succumb to a sexual obsession? After all, Anatole Zikos had promised repeatedly to end his relationship with Bastien's mother but somehow he had always ended up drifting back to Athene while coming up with one excuse after another. In truth Anatole had been too obsessed with Athene to ever give her up and her death had devastated him.

Leo was all too well aware that he was the son of almost neurotically volatile parents, who had remained locked in an emotional triangle of high drama throughout their marriage. His home life had been a nightmare and when he had visited his friends' homes he had marvelled at the quiet normality that they took for granted. When it came to what he viewed as his dodgy genes, Leo had always been relieved that he appeared to have skipped that over-emotional inheritance and was far too cold-blooded and logical to become obsessed with any woman. Indeed since his troubled childhood had taught him to mask his feelings and rigorously suppress or avoid any more intense reactions he had struggled to deal with any strong emotion.

But that approach wasn't likely to work for a male who had conceived a child with another woman in the run-up to his own wedding, Leo conceded bleakly. Everyone concerned had a right to strong emotions in a scenario like that. He had made the same mistake his father had—he had got the wrong woman pregnant. Wilfully or accidentally—did it matter which? Unlike his father, however, he would not compound his error by marrying a different woman and dragging her into the same shameful chaos. He had some tough decisions to make, he acknowledged grimly. It was no longer a matter of something as self-indulgent as what he *wanted*, but more a matter of honour. Such an old-fashioned word, that, Leo conceded ruefully, but if it meant that he accepted the need to put logic and fairness at the top of his list, it perfectly encapsulated his duty. And unlike his father, Leo planned to put his child first and foremost.

Around seven that same morning, Grace emerged from the shower, wrapped a fleecy towel round her nakedness and wondered ruefully where her cases were. Their frantic charge to the bedroom the night before had left no time for such niceties as unpacking. Her face burned and she glanced in one of the many mirrors, angry and ashamed of herself because she was still acting out of character and letting her life go off the rails. One mistake did not need to lead to another, so why had she slept with Leo again last night? Waking up in bed alone in the silent apartment with her brain awash with unfamiliar thoughts of self-loathing had unnerved her. Leo, she had decided miserably, Leo was *bad* for her.

She crept out to the hall where her luggage

still awaited her and she was about to lift a case when she heard a sound from another room and stiffened uncertainly.

'Grace…is that you?'

It was too late to retreat with any dignity but the discovery that Leo was still in the apartment and had not yet gone off to work as she had dimly assumed was unwelcome. She moved to the doorway of a large ultra-modern room flooded with light from a wall of windows and saw Leo. Her breath hitched in her throat. Barefoot, clad in only a pair of jeans unfastened at the waist and an unbuttoned shirt, Leo looked heartbreakingly gorgeous with his messy black hair, stubbled jawline and stunningly unreadable dark eyes gleaming in the sunlight.

'I thought you were out,' she confided. 'I need to get dressed.'

'No hurry… Housekeeping doesn't get here until nine.' Leo stared at her, his eyes eating her alive in the pounding silence. With her red hair rippling damply round her narrow shoulders, her triangular face warm with colour and her sea-glass eyes bright and evasive, she reminded him of a pixie. She was tiny and her curves were gloriously feminine. He wanted to tell her to drop the towel. The swelling at his groin was more than willing to bridge an awkward moment with sex.

'I have things to do.'

'Come here…I want to show you some properties,' Leo urged.

Grace moved reluctantly forward, one hand clutching the towel to her breasts lest it slip. She was wasting her time with the modesty, Leo thought helplessly. It only made him want to rip it off her more. 'Properties?' she questioned, dry-mouthed.

Leo sank down on the sofa he had abandoned and swung out the laptop he had been using. 'I've been looking for somewhere suitable for you to live.'

'But I'm here…er…I thought…'

'This is a company apartment, used by my father and my brother as well. It's serviced, convenient for me,' Leo explained. 'Until now

I haven't spent enough time in London to warrant the purchase of separate accommodation.'

'And that's changing?' Grace took a seat uneasily by his side and the faint but awesomely familiar scent of him assailed her nostrils, an intoxicating hint of sandalwood and citrus fruit with a foundation note of warm, musky masculinity. Below the towel her breasts beaded into straining points and warmth pooled in her pelvis.

'Obviously it will. If my child's going to be here, I will be too,' Leo countered carelessly, as if that truth was so obvious he shouldn't have to say it out loud. 'But fortunately I do own quite a few investment properties here and I've made up a small selection of the ones that are currently available for you.'

Grace was frowning in bewilderment. 'For... *me*?'

'You're homeless. My most basic responsibility should be ensuring that you have a comfortable and secure base.'

'I wasn't homeless until you persuaded me

to move out of Matt's spare room,' Grace said shortly, disliking the label as much as his take-charge attitude that suggested she was a problem to be tackled and solved. 'And I assumed I was staying *here*.'

'You need your own space.'

No, Leo wanted *his* space back, Grace suspected. Just then she recalled that he hadn't still been in bed with her the morning after their first night together on the yacht either. 'You should've left me where I was.'

'I'm not going to argue about this with you. It's futile,' Leo spelt out, flipping up the first of three luxury properties, chosen for proximity to her university campus.

Her lungs inflated while she listened to his spiel and watched the screen flip up properties that only someone wealthy could have afforded to rent. Her hands curled into fists and her soft mouth flattened over grinding teeth long before he reached the end of his running commentary and turned the laptop over to her for further perusal. It was the last straw. Grace sprang up and settled the laptop squarely back down on the coffee table. 'Thanks but no, thanks,' she said curtly.

Leo leapt up, his shirt flying back from his corrugated abdomen, his unsnapped waistband giving her a glimpse of the little black furrow of silky hair that arrowed down to his crotch. As she remembered how intimate she had been with him the night before the bottom seemed to fall out of her stomach and she felt positively ill with mortification.

'What the hell is that supposed to mean? That's *my* baby you're carrying and from now on until the finish line you're both *my* responsibility!' Leo shot back at her impatiently.

'No, I'm my own responsibility and I don't need a domineering, controlling man telling me what to do!' Grace flared instantly back at him, light green eyes glittering with the blistering anger she had been holding back. 'I understand that you want to stand by me to show me that you're a good guy but you're handing out very mixed messages and I prefer to know exactly where I stand.'

One look at her and Leo wanted her so badly at that moment that he physically hurt. Her passion called out to him on the deepest level of his psyche even though he had deliberately avoided that kind of passion all his life. She was having an emotional meltdown and that was all right, only to be expected, he told himself soothingly. 'If you were to stay with me, we'd end up in bed again and that's not a good idea when you don't yet know what your plans are.'

'I am not going to end up in bed with you again. I am *never* going to go to bed with you again!' Grace swore vehemently.

Far from comforted by that news, Leo groaned. 'Grace, you're a nice girl and I don't get involved with nice girls. I don't do love and romance. I can't be what you want if you want more.'

'I'm not going to be some kept woman in some house you own either, living off you like a leech because we had a stupid contraceptive accident!' Grace raked back at him furiously, infuriated to be called a 'nice girl' because that tag only suggested dreary, conservative and needy to her. In addition, although she refused to allow herself to dwell on her sense of rejection, she was horribly crushed by his cool, cynical disclaimer of any deeper feelings where she was concerned. 'I may be poor but I have my pride. You're interfering in my life far too much, Leo.'

Leo shocked himself by wanting to shout back at her. He wanted her to do what he told her to do, which was, after all, what ninety-nine per cent of the people in his life invariably did. Consequently, he very rarely, if ever, raised his voice. He was proud of his self-control but then he had always avoided emotional scenes, swiftly ditching women who specialised in them. Of course he had been raised by the ultimate of scene-throwers: his mother, whom he recalled staging dramatic walkouts, outrageous suicide threats and sobbing herself into hysterics.

'You have to have peace and quiet to continue your studies and decide what to do next. I'm *trying* not to interfere with that. If you weren't pregnant, you wouldn't be in this situation now. I only want what's best for you and the baby.'

'And the easiest thing for you to give is money,' Grace completed with reluctant comprehension, her troubled green eyes scanning the opulence of the furnishings and a view of the City of London that had to be next door to priceless. 'Isn't it?'

His lean, darkly handsome face tensed. 'Yes, so will you view the property you like the best? I'll have you moved in by the weekend. I think we should have dinner tonight and talk future options.'

'No, I have a student thing to attend,' Grace lied, freshly determined to dull her intense attraction to Leo by seeing less of him.

'Tomorrow night, then.'

'No, sorry.'

'Grace, I'm trying hard here,' Leo growled in warning.

'I have a check-up with the doctor booked.'

'I'll come with you and we'll eat afterwards,' Leo pronounced with satisfaction.

That wasn't what Grace wanted at all. She felt

like a ball being rolled down a steep hill in a direction she didn't want to go. Leo was getting much too involved in her life but by sleeping with him again hadn't she encouraged that? Torn in two by inner conflict, Grace lifted her chin. 'When do you want me to see this property?' she prompted.

'I have a board meeting this morning but late afternoon around four would suit me. I'll pick you up then.'

Grace wanted to tell him that she didn't need his escort either but it was *his* property and she could hardly object. All too frequently in life, Grace had discovered that necessity and practicality overruled any personal preference. Barring a return to Matt's guest room, she *was* technically homeless and in no position to dismiss an offer made by the father of her unborn child. She didn't like that truth but she had to live with it, she told herself unhappily.

When she emerged from the unused bedroom she had taken her case into, fully dressed and composed, Leo had left and Sheila, the friendly older woman washing the kitchen floor, asked her what she would like for breakfast. 'House-keeping' Leo had labelled Sheila with the casual indifference that spoke volumes about his privileged status in life. Grace ate cereal and toast at the kitchen table and learned all there was to know about Sheila's four adult children, grateful for the pleasant chatter that took her mind off her problems.

There was a tight, hard knot inside Grace's chest and it ached like mad. Over and over again she was still hearing Leo say, *I don't do love and romance...you're a nice girl.* Last night Leo had sung a very different tune, making her sound irresistible, giving her the heady impression that she meant more to him than she did while he smoothly talked her into an act of monumental stupidity. Of course, he had said all those things, demonstrated all that thrilling impatience *before* he got her into bed, and that told her all she really needed to know, didn't it? she scolded herself with newly learned cynicism. He had fooled her, manipulated her, got what he evidently wanted and then withdrawn behind boundaries again. There was a lesson to be learned there and she had learned it well.

A light knock sounded on the bedroom door while she was repacking her case. 'Grace...you have a visitor,' Sheila told her.

Bemused by the announcement when even Matt didn't have her address, Grace followed Sheila down to the hall to see a tall, very attractive brunette with a wealth of mahogany hair and dressed in a very fashionable outfit, who frowned at Grace in apparent astonishment. 'My goodness, you're not at all what I expected!' she exclaimed, extending a slim beringed hand. 'I'm Marina Kouros...and you can only be...*Grace*?'

CHAPTER SIX

'YES. AM I supposed to know who you are?' Grace asked the tall brunette awkwardly.

'Leo didn't mention me?' Marina Kouros prompted.

'I'm afraid not.'

'Coffee, Miss Kouros?' Sheila proffered from the kitchen doorway.

'No, thanks…we'll be in the sitting room,' the brunette said with easy authority, strolling confidently ahead of Grace, making it clear she knew her way around the apartment before she paused for an instant to firmly close the door.

'Why should Leo have mentioned you?' Grace asked stiffly as she hovered by the wall of windows, insanely conscious of her worn jeans and plain chain-store sweater when compared to her companion's expensive separates.

Marina's discomfiture was, for an instant, too obvious to be misinterpreted. 'Because Leo and I have been engaged for the past three years and we're getting married in six weeks' time…or, at least, we were until you came along.'

Grace's jaw felt frozen and unwieldy as she struggled to speak through underperforming facial muscles. *'Engaged?'* That single word was literally all she could squeeze out of her deflated lungs because her whole body felt as if it had gone into serious shock.

'I'll keep this brief. I'm not here to see you off…well, I suppose that's a lie. If you were to vanish into thin air right now, it would suit me very well, but I know you're pregnant and that it's not quite that simple.'

'Leo *told* you that I'm pregnant?' Grace whispered in even greater shock.

'He's very upfront like that but I must say you are a surprise. I was expecting a blonde bombshell with a pole dancer's wardrobe,' Marina admitted with a distressing candour that suggested Leo's infidelity was more normal than worthy of note. 'But look, I won't prevaricate. I'm here for one reason only. I don't want you to screw up Leo's life and mine and I was planning to offer you money to go away.'

Like an accident victim, Grace was frozen in place, her face as pale as milk, her eyes wide with consternation and haunted by too many powerful reactions to enumerate. Marina evoked so many different reactions in Grace; anger, mortification, guilt and pain were assailing her on all levels. Leo had lied to her. Leo had pretended to be single and unattached, and an engaged man on the brink of his wedding was anything but unattached. He had been engaged for *three* years? That was not a recent or a casual commitment.

'If Leo had told me he was engaged this wouldn't have happened because I would never have been with him in the first place,' Grace framed with desperate dignity. 'I'm genuinely sorry that anything I have done has upset you and that this situation is affecting you as well, but there is no way I would accept money from you.'

'I've known Leo all his life. He had a horrendous childhood and, because of it, he will never turn his back on his own child,' Marina informed her grimly. 'But I don't think he should have to sacrifice his whole life and all his plans *because* of that child. Somewhere, somehow there has to be a happy compromise for all of us.'

'I don't know what to say to you,' Grace framed sickly, her mind glossing over that reference to Leo's childhood because she could barely cope as it was with the overload of information and thoughts already bombarding her. 'I don't know what I can say…other than, how can you still care about a man who cheats on you?'

'I think that's my business.'

'Just as the baby's mine,' Grace countered quietly. 'I don't know what you want from me, Marina. But I won't be staying on in this apartment.'

'I only want you to think about what you're doing. *If* you have that baby…' Marina breathed with unmistakeable bitterness, her well-mannered mask slipping without warning '…you're wrecking *all* our lives!'

'But that's my decision to make,' Grace pointed out with wooden precision as she battled her churning inner turmoil to walk back to the door Marina had closed. She opened the door again in unapologetic invitation. 'If you're finished, I don't think we have anything else to say to each other right now.'

Across the city, Leo said a very bad word below his breath when he read the warning text from Marina. For the first time ever he was really furious with his ex, his quick and clever brain instantly envisaging the potential fallout from what Grace had just discovered about him. Grace already had quite enough on her plate without that and Marina had absolutely no right to interfere. Had Marina hit out at Grace in revenge? Having always trusted his oldest and most loyal friend, Leo was taken aback by the suspicion, but the timing of Marina's visit spoke for itself and could hardly be deemed an accident. His handsome mouth twisted and he stood up at the board table to excuse himself from the meeting; he *had* to see Grace before she did something stupid.

That was the most surprising thing about Grace, which he had quickly registered. She might have a very clever brain and a steel backbone of independence but both were combined with an alarming tendency to make very sudden decisions and execute moves that were not always wise. It was that deeply buried vein of spontaneous passion and adventure in Grace that worried Leo the most. How else did he explain that night on his yacht? After almost twenty-five years of being a virgin she had just picked him like a rabbit out of a hat? A man about whom she knew nothing? Leo was still appalled by the risk she had taken on him that night until it occurred to him that he had never expended a similar amount of anxiety on any other casual sex partner. Only then did he crack down hard on his undesirable feelings of concern and the vague suspicion that Grace was much more fragile and vulnerable than she liked to pretend.

Well, once they were married, he wouldn't

need to worry about her any longer. He would know where she was, what she was doing…in short, once he had control of Grace, *full* control, the horrible sense of apprehension that had gripped him since he first learned of her pregnancy would die a natural death. His anxiety was undoubtedly focused on the baby, he told himself consolingly. The baby was only a speck barely visible to the naked eye at this stage of his or her development—Leo had looked it up on the Internet—but it was *his* future son or daughter and he knew that baby was virtually defenceless and utterly dependent on the health and well-being of its mother's body for survival. What the hell had Marina been thinking of when she had deliberately approached a woman in Grace's condition to break such bad news? Hadn't she appreciated how dangerous that could be?

Grace was stacking her luggage in the hall when the front door opened again. She had been frantically struggling to get herself out of the apartment as fast as possible while accepting the demeaning truth that she could not afford to call a taxi to ferry her and her possessions away in one go. No, she would have to leave stuff to be collected at a later date. But most threatening of all was the awareness that she had absolutely no place else to go because a return to Matt's flat, Matt, who had been constantly texting her with revealing urgency since her departure, was definitely not an option.

As Grace straightened Leo stepped through the door and snapped it shut behind him without removing his glittering dark eyes from her once. 'Going somewhere?' he asked shortly.

Grace hadn't seen Leo leave earlier. In a navy pinstripe suit that screamed designer elegance and a plain white shirt teamed with a jazzy red tie, Leo looked absolutely stunning. Her heartbeat quickened as she remembered running her fingers through his black hair the night before and the unforgettable taste of his mouth. Heat was beginning to stir inside her when she shut down hard on that response, fighting that potent physical pull with all her might, reminding herself of what he was and denying it until she was back in control again.

Grace lifted her chin. 'Yes, somewhere as far as possible from you,' she answered.

'Marina told me she'd come to see you.' His beautiful shapely lips compressed, a muscle pulling tight at the corner of his unsmiling mouth. 'She shouldn't have done that.'

'Oh, I don't know,' Grace fielded in a tremulous driven undertone that mortified her, frankly bemused by a relationship that crossed the expected boundaries. It was inconceivable to her that Marina would've told Leo she had been to see Grace. 'Considering the way you've behaved I thought she was remarkably restrained in what she had to say.'

'My relationship with Marina is not as straightforward as you probably assume it is. Nor does what it entailed matter now because I *broke off* our engagement earlier today.' Leo studied her with screened intensity, expecting an immediate lessening of the tension in the atmosphere.

Grace refused to react in any way because

that announcement did not lessen her sense of betrayal in the slightest. 'You said you were single…you *lied*,' she condemned with quiet simplicity.

'Let's move this out of the hall and talk like grown-ups,' Leo suggested grittily.

'I've got nothing to say to you, Leo, so I suggest we stay where we are and you let me leave.'

'Diavelos…' Leo ground out, his frustration finally bubbling over in response to her pale composed expression and cold light green eyes. He had expected to find Grace distraught. Somehow he had expected her to shout and sob because he knew, or he had thought he knew, that like some chocolates she had a soft inner centre and would be hurt about what she had learned about him. Instead he was looking at a disturbingly controlled young woman, who refused to either shout or sob, and he didn't know how to deal with that at all. 'In the circumstances you *must* have something to say to me.'

'But I doubt very much if you want to hear it.' So great was the strain of maintaining her tough, unfeeling façade, Grace could barely speak. Pain and disillusionment sat like a massive block inside her chest, radiating toxic, wounding rays of insecurity, hurt and rejection. He had devastated her, shattered her heart into a hundred pieces, but on another level she was grateful for Marina's visit because at least she had found Leo out for the rat he was before she became any more deeply involved with him.

Leo thrust the door of the sitting room so wide that it bounced back noisily. 'I *do* want to hear it!' he challenged.

Reckoning that he was going to make it difficult for her to leave without a muck-raking confrontation and marvelling that he could even want that, Grace trudged into the big room where Marina had faced her with the truth that had destroyed her dreams. Silly, sentimental, romantic dreams, utterly inappropriate dreams for a woman of her age, intelligence and background to have cherished: the dream that a man could be decent and honest and trustworthy.

With her parents' history before her, she

should've known better, Grace thought painfully. Even her own father had lied and cheated rather than keep his promise to marry her mother. Soon after Grace's birth, her father had begun working with the woman who would eventually become his first wife and he had kept his infidelity a secret while continuing to live with Grace and her mother. She had the vaguest possible memory of her father because he had walked out on her mother before Grace reached her second birthday.

Grace spun round to face Leo, her arms folded defensively across her slightly built body. 'Right, exactly what do you want from me? Forgiveness? Understanding? Well, sorry, you're not getting either!' she told him roundly.

'I want to explain.'

'No, I don't want to hear any explanations… a bit pointless at this stage!' Grace pointed out curtly. 'You lied to me and there's no getting round that. Don't waste any more of my time, Leo. Let me go.'

'To go where?'

'I don't know yet.' Grace was distracted by the buzzing of her mobile phone in the back pocket of her jeans and she dug it out and switched it off, noticing in forgivable surprise that it was her aunt calling her. Considering her aunt had told her never to bother her family again, what could she possibly want? Unless her uncle Declan, who had visited Grace at Matt's flat, had persuaded his wife to soften her attitude.

'You can't leave when you don't have anywhere to go!' Leo argued fiercely. 'You have to take care of yourself now that you're pregnant!'

'Oh, please, don't pretend you actually *care*,' Grace countered with withering sarcasm, her bitterness licking out from below the surface before she could prevent it from showing.

'If you would just listen to me and stop being so unreasonable,' Leo bit out.

'I don't need to listen. I already know what you are and that's a dirty, lying, cheating scumbag without an ounce of integrity!' Grace shot at him, green eyes suddenly flaring bright as angry stars because he had dared to call *her* unreasonable.

'I broke off my engagement so that I could come back here and ask you to marry me!' Leo launched at her in outrage, fury surging up inside him like lava inside a volcano about to erupt. He had never felt so angry in his life and it was an unnerving experience. He didn't get angry; he didn't *do* angry. Nothing and no one had ever been capable of sending him over that edge because to get angry you had to care and he was not supposed to care.

Grace slowly shook her head at him in apparent wonderment, an attitude that enraged Leo even more because no woman had ever dared to look at him like that. 'Well, the answer to that proposal would've been a very firm no once I found out what you had been hiding from me. Honesty and reliability are hugely important to me, Leo, and you score nil on both counts. I saw today what you did to Marina and I'm afraid that was quite enough to convince me that you're a very arrogant, selfish personality with very few saving graces…no pun intended.'

'Is that all you've got to say to my suggestion that we get married?' Leo growled, hardly able to credit what he was hearing because nobody, least of all a woman, had ever found him wanting on *any* score. So prejudiced against him was Grace that it almost felt to him as though she saw some mirror image of him that was another person entirely. And then he remembered her history and somewhere inside his head an alarm bell clanged, putting him right on target.

'Yes, that's all I've got to say. Once the baby's born, I'll get in touch with you at this address,' Grace assured him flatly. 'But be warned…I have no plans to hand my child over to you or anything like that because you're not my idea of a father in any way.'

Leo could literally feel himself freezing into an ice pillar while still wanting to strangle her into silence. Did he deserve such a character assassination? Well, so much for the winning power of a marriage proposal and a rich and powerful husband! But offended and infuriated as he was by Grace and the awareness that he had seriously underestimated her temper, he was more fixated on where she planned to go when she appeared to have neither money nor any suitable friends or family to live with. Recognising that Grace needed to cool off before he could even hope to reason with her, he reached into his wallet to withdraw a card and extended it.

'I own the hotel. It's small and discreet and you only need to show the card at Reception to be accommodated. My driver will take you there…'

In the grip of frantic thought and the blistering emotional turmoil that their encounter had provoked, Grace accepted the card. She had to go somewhere and she had no place else, she thought wretchedly, and ditched her pride. 'OK.'

A shard of relief speared through Leo's almost overwhelming sense of rage and raw frustration. She wouldn't listen to him, she refused to listen, refused to let him talk…how fair was that? He hated feeling powerless, an unfamiliar sensation because she was the only person who had ever had that effect on him. Even so, it was of paramount importance to Leo that he knew where she was and that she was safe and well looked after. She had got him wrong, *so* wrong, he thought bitterly.

In Leo's limo, Grace dug out her phone to check it and called back her aunt.

'I need to see you urgently,' Della Donovan said in an unusually constrained voice.

Grace wondered what on earth had happened to make her aunt approach her because she was fairly certain that Jenna's dislike of her had initially been learned from her mother. Compressing her lips, she agreed to meet up for coffee that afternoon. Had her uncle pressured his wife into burying the hatchet and healing the breach? The suspicion worried her. Declan Donovan was a kind man but, sadly, such feelings couldn't be forced.

The hotel was small, unassuming from the outside but the last word in elegant opulence and service on the inside. Within minutes of her presenting the card, her luggage was collected and she was settled in a large and beautiful room complete with every possible luxury. The bathroom was a dream and as soon as she had unpacked Grace laid out clean clothes for her meeting with her aunt and went for a bath in an effort to relax her sadly frayed nerves.

She felt so unhappy. In all her life, Grace had never felt quite so unhappy. She had always been alone but she had never felt lonelier than she did at that moment, cut off from everything familiar and at her third change of address in the space of a week. The following week term started and she would be back in class and facing hospital placements. But for the first time ever Grace wasn't looking forward to getting back to her studies. The events of the past worrying weeks had taken their toll and she was exhausted.

Leo had broken off his engagement so that he could ask her to marry him. A sudden involuntary surge of tears stung Grace's gritty eyes. Only now was her brain calmed enough to consider that truth. He was trying so hard to do the right thing even though he had started out doing the wrong thing by not telling her that he was engaged. Did she give him points for that? Grace heaved a heavy sigh. She had been falling in love with him, weaving dreams, seeing a future that might include him, and then Marina had blown that fantasy out of the water. Marina had spelt out the reality that Leo had not only lied to Grace, but was also a regular playboy. That crack Marina had made in which she admitted having expected Grace to be a blonde bombshell in a pole dancer's outfit had lingered longest with Grace. Evidently Leo had betrayed his fiancée more than once. He was a liar and a cheat just like her father, who had also turned out to be a great deal less interested in raising his own child than he had first pretended to be.

Della Donovan was seated in a corner of the busy coffee shop when Grace arrived. She was immaculate in a smart suit, her blonde hair in a chignon; her critical gaze scanned her niece in her trademark jeans. And for the first time ever, Grace felt like picking up on that faintly scornful appraisal and asking when she had ever had the money to dress as smartly as the rest of the family. She suppressed the urge, recognising that now that she had moved out of her aunt's home, where she had always had to watch every word to keep the peace, such humility no longer came naturally to her.

'Grace...' Della murmured with a rather forced smile. 'How have you been?'

And to Grace's astonishment, her aunt engaged her in polite small talk.

'You said this was urgent,' Grace finally reminded the older woman, wondering what the heck was holding her aunt back from simply saying whatever it was she wanted to say.

'I'm afraid I have to ask you a rather personal question first.' Her aunt pursed her lips. 'Is Leos Zikos the father of your child?'

'That's private—' Grace began.

'Oh, for goodness' sake, I wouldn't be asking if it wasn't important!' Della snapped, for the first time sounding like her usual self.

'Yes...he is,' Grace confirmed grudgingly.

The older woman paled. 'I was hoping I was wrong because I was very rude to him and even ruder when he asked for you.'

Grace was unsurprised. 'I'm sure he'll get over it.'

'A man that rich and influential doesn't have to get *over* anything!' Della Donovan argued in a fierce undertone. 'Leos Zikos owns the company your uncle works for. He channels work for that company through the legal firm *I* work for. You're far from stupid, Grace. The father of your baby has a huge amount of power over your family and if you don't keep him sweet, he could punish *all* of us.'

It was a bittersweet moment for Grace, hearing herself described as part of the family for the very first time, but she was thoroughly disconcerted by the genuine apprehension she could see in Della's anxious face. 'You're seriously worried about that risk?'

'Of course I am. Zikos has a name for being hard, ruthless and unforgiving and I'm asking you to smooth things over with him for your family's sake.'

Grace realised why she was being temporarily promoted to family status and almost laughed. 'Della, Leo hasn't ever mentioned either you or Declan.'

Unimpressed, Della curled her lip. 'We looked after you when you were a child, Grace. Now I expect you to look after us and ensure that there is no reason for Leo Zikos to sack your uncle from his job or withdraw business from my legal firm. After all, it's *your* fault that I was brusque with him… I know I offended him but he arrived in the middle of a family crisis… Make sure he understands that.'

Grace was astonished by the entire tenor of the conversation. Della was scared that her comfortable life was under threat. Only genuine anxiety on that score would have persuaded the older woman to meet up with her despised niece and ask her for help to smooth over any offence caused. Grace thought it best not to mention that she was currently at serious odds with

Leo herself, having called him a lying, cheating scumbag without integrity.

'I'll check out the situation for you and, if necessary, explain things,' Grace promised to bring the uncomfortable meeting to an end. 'But I really don't think you have anything to worry about.'

'Grace, you have about as much idea as to how the very wealthy *expect* to be treated as a farm animal!' her aunt told her with raw-edged impatience.

Back at the hotel, Grace ordered a meal from room service and lay on the bed, pondering that strange encounter. She believed that her aunt was panicking without good cause. But hadn't she already discovered that she did not know Leo as well as she had assumed? It was not a situation she could ignore, was it? Leo could well be the vengeful type when people crossed him. Della had probably been very rude to him: Della in a temper didn't hold back. As Grace thrust her tray away, she lifted her phone, her conscience twanging. She couldn't simply ignore her aunt's fears simply because she herself did not want to speak to Leo.

'Grace…' Leo growled down the phone like a grizzly bear, apparently not in any better a mood than when she had last seen him.

'I need to talk to you,' Grace advanced stiffly.

'I'll be with you in an hour.' At the other end of the phone, Leo smiled with a strong sense of satisfaction. Clearly, Grace had calmed down and finally seen sense. Nobody was perfect. He had made *one* mistake. And she needed him, of course she did; he was the father of her baby…

An hour later, a knock sounded on the door and Grace used the peephole, recognising one of Leo's bodyguards before opening the door. 'Yes?'

'The boss is on the top floor waiting for you,' she was told.

Grace grabbed her key card and followed the man into the lift. Of course, if Leo owned the place he would have an office or something in the building, she guessed. She breathed in slow and deep at the thought of seeing Leo again.

She could handle it; she could handle him without letting herself down. Couldn't she? She had never been one of those girls who was a pushover for a good-looking, smooth-tongued male, although to be honest, she reasoned, she had met none before Leo, which meant that Leo kind of reigned supreme in her imagination as the ultimate player.

She smoothed damp palms down over the denim skirt she had teamed with a green T-shirt. Dressing up for him? That suspicion was a joke when she recalled how Marina had looked, all glossy and glitzy with wonderfully smooth straight hair and amazing make-up. No bad fairy had cursed Marina at birth with red curly hair and freckles, not to mention breasts and hips that would have suited someone much taller.

She walked into a beautifully decorated large room. It had a bed like hers but there the similarity ended because it was much more of a five-star suite. Leo was by the window, broad, straight shoulders taut with a tension she could feel, and in spite of her inner strictures her heart leapt even before he swung round to face her.

'Grace…' he said and his dark deep drawl shimmied down her spine with the potent sexual charisma that was so much a part of him.

Leo felt a hard-on kick in as he focused momentarily on the swell of Grace's high, full breasts below the thin top and the slender perfection of the thighs he hadn't had a good look at since they first met. *Diavelos*, he loved her body, he really, *really* loved her body. It just did it for him every time the way no other woman's ever had. He looked and he simply wanted to touch, taste, *take*.

'I wanted to see you to discuss something… probably something you'll consider quite silly,' Grace warned him uncomfortably, striving to not quite focus on his lean, darkly handsome features with a mouth running dry and a tummy turning somersaults. But there he was, gorgeous, no denying that, she conceded helplessly while she fought to concentrate on what she had to say.

Leo had the celebratory champagne standing

by on ice. He knew she was pregnant but was convinced that one little sip would do no harm simply to mark the occasion, because of course she wanted to see him to tell him that she was ready to marry him. The true celebration would be taking her back to bed again, knowing she was his...*finally*. When it dawned on him that Grace was burbling on for some strange reason about her uncle's job and her aunt's legal firm, he was perplexed, until the proverbial penny dropped and he made the necessary leap of understanding. Of course, what else would a lying, cheating scumbag do but throw his weight around through threats and intimidation?

'And you're afraid that I took offence?' Leo prompted, taking very much more offence from what she was saying than from anything her shrewish aunt had thrown at him.

'Yes, of course, I know you're not really like that...' Grace assured him.

No, you don't know. They wouldn't be having this conversation if she knew him and without warning a scorching tide of rage was washing over Leo like a dangerous floodtide.

Grace stared at Leo, noticing that his big powerful body had gone very, very still. His dark eyes shone as bright as gold ingots below his lush black lashes.

'They're my family…I do *care* about what happens to them,' Grace framed in uncertain continuation. 'They really don't deserve to be dragged into this mess between us.'

'I won't adversely affect their lives in any way *if* you agree to marry me,' Leo delivered in a tone that brought gooseflesh to her bare arms.

'I beg your pardon?'

'I think you heard me, Grace. If you do what I want and marry me, I will promise not to interfere with your uncle and aunt's continuing employment.'

Before his shrewd, hard gaze, Grace turned white. 'You can't mean that, not that you would seriously threaten their livelihoods just because *I'm* not doing what you want?'

'I *mean* it,' Leo asserted with fierce emphasis.

'I've run out of patience. I want to marry you and I want that child you're carrying. So, think very carefully about what *you* decide to do next.'

'But that's complete blackmail!' Grace shot back at him, trembling like a leaf in shock and barely able to credit what he was telling her.

'I never pretended to be a knight on a white horse, Grace. You and that baby are *mine* and the sooner you acknowledge that, the happier we will all be.'

'I don't belong to anyone. I belong to myself,' Grace argued through gritted teeth, battling a terrifying sense of panic as hard as she could because Leo had just trashed the faith she hadn't known she still cherished in him.

Leo stalked closer, well over six feet of powerfully built and determined masculinity. 'That was before you met me, *meli mou.* Everything's changed now. We'll get married on Friday.'

'Fri-Friday is only three days away,' Grace stammered, utterly thrown by Leo's controlling behaviour.

'I know and I can't wait to sign on that official

dotted line,' Leo grated impatiently. 'Then I'll know *where* you are and *how* you are.'

'You're out of your mind,' Grace breathed in a daze. 'We can't just get married. You were engaged to Marina!'

'Marina's the past, you're the present,' Leo cut in with ruthless bite. 'And at this moment I'm only interested in the future and it starts here, *now* with your answer...'

Grace pinned tremulous lips together in the terrible stretching silence. Her heart seemed to be hammering in her eardrums. He was threatening her aunt and uncle's comfortable life and she couldn't just stand by and do nothing after all they had done for her, she thought wretchedly. They had brought her up, supported her at school, kept her safe. All right, it had been far from perfect but they were still the only family she had and she didn't want them to suffer in any way by association with her. Leo held all the cards: her uncle's employment, Della's legal firm's dependency on the business Leo sent their way. Della had worked long and hard for a partnership and if she had been rude to Leo—well, she was pretty rude to a lot of people, never having been the type to tolerate fools. Grace's mind and her thoughts were in turmoil.

'You could explain now about Marina,' she proffered tersely.

'No, that ship's already sailed,' Leo slammed back at her coolly. 'Are you marrying me on Friday or not?'

Grace wanted to say not, to puncture his carapace of arrogant strength and challenge him, but her character was grounded very firmly in compassion and the risk of her relatives having to pay a high price for her mistake in getting pregnant by the wrong man was not one she could ignore. She snatched in a wavering breath and damned him with her pale green defiant gaze. 'I'll give you an answer in the morning.'

'Why drag this out?'

'Because it's a very big decision,' Grace countered quietly. 'I'll tell you what I've decided tomorrow.'

Impatience assailed Leo and he gritted his

strong white teeth. Her eyes were luminous pools of pale green but he noticed the dark circles etched below them and her general pallor. 'You look very tired.'

Grace coloured in receipt of that unflattering comment. 'I'm going back downstairs to go straight to bed.'

'Have you eaten?' he shot at her as she reached the door.

'Yes,' she said.

'I'll meet you here for breakfast at eight in the morning,' Leo decreed.

How could she marry a man who had been planning to marry another woman for three long years? How could she surrender to blackmail? Would Leo really damage her aunt's and uncle's livelihoods and careers? Or was he bluffing? And if bluffing was a possibility was she prepared to light the fuse and wait and see what actually happened if she said no?

Grace lay in bed mulling over those weighty questions. Although she had completely dismissed the idea, Leo had mentioned marriage the very first day he'd discovered she was pregnant, she recalled ruefully. It seemed that marrying the mother of his child was important to him, *so* important he had immediately recognised it as a necessity. Not that that excused him in any way for employing threats when persuasion had failed, she reasoned.

Grace had so many unanswered questions that she was now wishing that she had listened to what Leo had had to say for himself earlier that day at his apartment. Clearly, Leo's relationship with Marina was unusual. When Marina had introduced herself to Grace, she had been fairly polite and remarkably composed for a female whose fiancé had just dumped her for another woman. Even so, Marina had repeatedly said that Grace having Leo's child would wreck *all* their lives. It was possible that Marina was simply a good actress but even that didn't explain the peculiarity of Marina visiting Grace to try and buy her off and then freely admitting that embarrassing fact to Leo.

Her head beginning to pound with the strain

of her anxious reflections, Grace acknowledged that had Marina not existed she would've agreed to marry Leo. After all, it was best to be honest with herself: she did *want* Leo in spite of the shocks he had dealt her. It wasn't sensible, it wasn't justifiable but she had pretty much been infatuated with Leo from the moment she'd met him. On those grounds and bearing in mind the reality that she would very much like her baby to grow up with a father, shouldn't she give marriage a chance?

Only, how did she marry a male willing to blackmail her into agreement? That was wrong, that was *so* wrong. And the best of it was, she was convinced that Leo *knew* it was wrong but he had still put that pressure on her in an effort to get what he wanted. She did owe a debt of care to her uncle and aunt and if their lives were blighted because of something she had done she would be gutted, which didn't give her much in the way of choice. On the other hand, Grace reflected as she swallowed another yawn, she could agree to marriage with certain provisos attached.

* * *

Leo studied Grace as she joined him for breakfast, her face blank, her eyes uninformative. He reckoned she would make a good poker player and the challenge of that talent in a potential wife amused him. 'Well?' he prompted grimly, still annoyed that she had forced him to wait for her answer.

Grace sipped at her tea, wishing that Leo didn't look quite so amazing first thing in the morning when she felt washed out and weary. There he was with his dark golden eyes alive with potent leaping energy, his blue-black hair still damp from the shower and his hard jawline close shaven. He wore yet another one of those remarkably well-tailored suits that beautifully defined his lean, muscular build. 'I'll say yes because you really haven't given me a choice.'

'Choice is a very much overrated gift,' Leo declared, pouring himself a cup of fragrant coffee with a steady hand, determined not to react in any way to her capitulation. 'People don't always make the *right* choice. Sometimes they need a little push in the relevant direction.'

'This was more than a little push,' Grace censured. 'I don't know why you're doing it either. You can't want me as a wife that much.'

'Why not?'

'I'm just ordinary.'

'I don't see you that way, *meli mou*,' Leo countered. 'I see you as different, as special.'

'Leo, you just blackmailed me into marrying you. Ditch the flattery!' Grace said very drily. 'And I may be saying yes but there would have to be certain conditions attached.'

Leo tensed again and flung back his arrogant head, shapely mouth flattening back into a tough line. 'Such as?'

'As the term hasn't started yet, I'm considering taking a year out while all this is going on but I would want to return to my studies in London next year. You would have to support that.'

'Naturally I would support that arrangement,' Leo asserted, the tension locking his lean bronzed features into tautness evaporating.

Grace went pink and gathered her strength. 'And it would have to be a platonic marriage.'

Leo went rigid again and studied her with incredulous dark eyes as if she were insane. 'You can't be serious?'

'Of course, I'm serious. We don't have to be intimate to be married and raise a child together.'

His dark golden gaze rested on her resolute face. 'I'm afraid you do if you're married to me. I refuse to look outside my marriage for sex. That would degrade both of us and I couldn't live with it. I have strong views on fidelity,' he completed with finality.

Grace groaned out loud, not having expected him to be quite so set against what would in effect have been a marriage only on paper. 'I really did think that that would be the sensible option.'

'No, it would be a recipe for disaster.' Leo stared at her with his black-lashed dark eyes glittering like stars in a lean, angular face that was so handsome it made the breath trip in her tight throat. 'And I speak from experience. My father was persistently unfaithful to my mother and their unhappiness poisoned life for both them and their children.'

'My goodness…' Taken aback by that unexpectedly frank admission, Grace regrouped as she finished eating. 'But it wouldn't be quite so personal with us. For a start, we're not in love with each other or anything like that.'

'But I still want you, Grace, as a man wants a woman,' Leo delivered with savage candour. 'I won't pretend otherwise. I want a normal marriage with all that that entails, not some unnatural agreement that increases the odds of divorce. I also *want* to be there for our child as he or she grows up.'

'You've made your point,' Grace conceded grudgingly, willing to admit that she had not thought through the consequences of a platonic marriage. It had been naïve to assume that Leo might be willing to live without sex while the alternative of her having to turn a blind eye while Leo sought sexual consolation elsewhere was even less appealing to her. But how could he say that he had strong views on fidelity after what he had done to Marina?

As she pushed her plate away and stood up, her curiosity still fully engaged on the mystery of Leo's thought processes, Leo stood up as well.

'So, we're getting married in forty-eight hours?' Leo mused huskily, resting a hand on her arm.

'I think that's a yes.' Still striving to keep her distance, Grace tried to gently detach her arm from his hold but she didn't act fast enough because his other arm just closed round her spine to entrap her slim body against his lean, powerful frame. He was hard…*everywhere*. Hard-packed with muscle, tense and…fully erect. Her face burned in the split second before his mouth came crashing down on hers, nibbling, licking, tasting in a carnal assault on her senses that absolutely no other man could have contrived. Her head fell back and her mouth opened, treacherous excitement lighting her up like a shower of fireworks inside. It was so incredibly sexy. In a mindless moment she was convinced it was the sexiest kiss ever.

A knock sounded on the door and he pulled back from her. A waiter brought in champagne. Flustered by the power of that compellingly provocative kiss and shaken by the thought that she was actually going to marry Leo, Grace backed away to the window to practise breathing again.

Leo extended a champagne flute to her. 'To our future.'

'I shouldn't drink.'

'One sip for the sake of it,' Leo suggested.

Grace touched the flute to her mouth, moistening her lips.

'I'll set up a shopping trip for you today. You need clothes.' Unusually, Leo hesitated. 'Marina has offered to help out.'

'Marina?' Grace exclaimed, wide-eyed.

'We're still good friends. She's probably feeling a bit guilty that she approached you yesterday to buy you off because that sort of behaviour really isn't her style,' Leo remarked with a wry roll of his eyes. 'What you see is what you get with Marina. But if you would feel uncomfortable with her, I'll make a polite excuse…'

In the taut silence, Grace swallowed with difficulty, her mind functioning at top speed. Leo's ex-fiancée was offering to assist her in preparing for their shotgun wedding out of a genuine desire to be helpful? Grace's curiosity about the unconventional nature of Marina's relationship with Leo literally shot into the stratosphere at that revelation. Evidently their ties of friendship had withstood the breaking off of the engagement and the bitterness that Marina had briefly revealed, and that more than anything else impressed Grace and made her want to know more.

'No, don't make an excuse. It's an unusual situation but I think that Marina's kind gesture should be met with equal generosity,' Grace pronounced, hoping that she was making the right decision and not setting herself up as a target for the sort of spiteful comments of the type her cousin and her aunt had specialised in.

CHAPTER SEVEN

'FROM A PRACTICAL point of view, I've been up to my throat in wedding arrangements for the past few weeks, so I know exactly what I'm doing and who to contact,' Marina proffered as she sat beside Grace in the back of Leo's opulent limousine an hour later.

'But there isn't enough time to organise anything fancy.'

'When a man is as rich as Leo is, there are always people willing to meet a challenge for a substantial bonus,' the brunette told her drily.

'But why should *you* help us?' Grace asked baldly, no longer able to swallow back that burning and obvious question.

'I have my pride. First and foremost, I would prefer our friends to believe that the break-up was amicable rather than inspire a pity party,'

Marina fielded wryly. 'I've also since had a radical rethink about my own future. Yesterday when I went to meet you I was fighting to preserve the status quo but, having cooled down, I'm now more inclined to think that Leo and I were just treading water and never meant to be. My father is deeply disappointed that he's not getting his dream whiz-kid son-in-law but I'm afraid I want to do what's right for me.'

'You're being very understanding.'

Marina laughed. 'Not as understanding as you probably think. To be frank, I have someone else in my life too and I believe that eventually Zack will make me happier than Leo ever would have done.'

Grace absorbed that unexpected admission without visible reaction. Yet it was undeniably a relief for her to learn that the svelte brunette was not the innocent and cruelly betrayed fiancée Grace had initially assumed she was. 'Even so, you and Leo still seem to be very close.'

'But there was always a flaw in our relationship.' Marina turned to look at Grace with a self-mocking light in her lively dark eyes. 'Although most men consider me attractive Leo never wanted me the way he wanted you.'

'I can't believe that,' Grace said uncomfortably, her face burning with sudden heat.

Marina grimaced. 'It's true and his detachment was bad for my ego. However, because we were friends from a young age, Leo believed we were an ideal match.'

'But you must've loved Leo as well,' Grace incised, cutting through the brunette's frustratingly guarded comments.

'Oh, yes, when I was younger I was absolutely mad about Leo! He was the full package—gorgeous, successful, strong—everything I wanted in a future husband,' the other woman admitted with a rueful laugh. 'Unfortunately, though, when it mattered I never made the girlfriend cut: Leo kept me firmly in the "friends" category. And when he suggested that we get married, I refused to listen to what he was saying and chose to assume that I meant more to him than he was willing to admit.' Her expressive lips compressed. 'Only I couldn't have been more wrong. He didn't mislead me, but any romantic feelings I once cherished for Leo were withered by his indifference.'

'He hurt you and yet you've forgiven him,' Grace commented in surprise.

Marina shrugged as she led the way into a designer bridal boutique. 'Life's too short for anything else. Just be sure you know what you're getting into with Leo because I doubt very much that he'll change.'

A small posse of assistants were waiting to greet them. Grace was extracted from her coat while Marina spoke to the designer, an effervescent blonde. Grace posed like a small statue while she was measured and wondered if she did have the slightest idea what she was getting into in choosing to marry Leo. Evidently he hadn't ever been in love with Marina. Furthermore Marina had ultimately found someone else to love as well, which was what made it possible for the brunette to civilly accept the bride Leo was taking in her place.

'Surely it doesn't matter what I wear to a civil ceremony?' Grace whispered to Marina.

'It will be your first appearance as Leo's wife and you'll feel more confident if you're properly turned out,' Marina asserted sagely. 'Being badly dressed won't impress anyone.'

'I don't really care about impressing people,' Grace admitted.

'But in our world, whether you like it or not, appearances *do* matter,' Marina traded without apology. The designer remarked that white and cream drained Grace of colour and tested less orthodox shades against her skin. Even Grace recognised *the* dress when it was held against her, an unconventional choice that provided an amazingly flattering background for her vibrant hair and pale complexion.

And as the seemingly endless day wore on with a lengthy trip to Harrods and the additional services of a very helpful fashion stylist, Grace discovered that she liked, possibly even *loved*, expensive, well-made clothes. Her fingers smoothed the softest cashmere, stroked silk and traced the delicate patterns of lace and exquisite embroidery. Astonishment and growing awe gripped her when those pricey designer garments shaped her figure and made her look so much better than she had ever dreamt she could look. When the overwhelming shopping experience was finally finished she slid her feet into comfy little pumps teamed with a short black skirt and a zingy sapphire-blue jacket and studied her sleek and elegant reflection in positive stupefaction. For the first time ever Grace thought she looked pretty and that maybe a spot of cosmetic enhancement would help even more.

'Thanks for everything,' she murmured with heartfelt gratitude to Marina, who had waved a magic wand over her like a fairy godmother bent on transforming Cinderella.

'Tomorrow you hit the beauty salon for some treatments and you won't be thanking me then. You haven't ever even plucked your eyebrows, have you?' the brunette prompted in a mixture of amusement and fascination.

Grace winced. 'Is it that obvious?'

Marina laughed. 'Comfort yourself with the knowledge that, in spite of your laissez-faire attitude in the grooming stakes, Leo admitted he couldn't take his eyes off you the first time he saw you.'

'He actually *told* you that?' Grace prompted, colour flaring in her pale cheeks.

Marina nodded confirmation. 'At least he was honest.'

Back at the hotel, Grace went straight up to the suite Leo was using. A stranger opened the door and two others were hovering round the desk at which Leo sat, his jacket off, his tie loosened, broad shoulder muscles flexing below a white silk shirt as he turned his head and stared fixedly at Grace where she hovered, uncertain of her welcome.

He sprang upright. 'Marina did good,' he quipped, brilliant dark golden eyes sliding over her slim figure in a look as physical as a touch. 'In fact, she did brilliantly.'

'She was a tremendous help.' Grace's colour was heightened by his scrutiny and the disturbing reaction of her body to that unashamedly sexual appraisal. Her nipples had prickled into taut sensitivity while a drenching pool of heat settled between her thighs. She was shaken by the intensity of her desire for him to reach out and touch her.

'My staff…' Leo introduced the three men before swiftly dismissing them. The trio swiftly gathered up laptops, briefcases and jackets and filed out. 'I need to have a word with you about the guest list for the wedding,' he told her levelly.

When asked earlier, Grace had put down Matt and her uncle's family but could think of no one else to include and she studied him enquiringly.

'I take it, then…that you've decided not to invite your father?' Leo pressed, sharply disconcerting her.

'How could I? I've never met him, n-never had any contact with him.' In confusion and shock at the unexpected question, Grace stumbled over her words, wondering how he even knew that she had a father alive.

'Never?'

'Not since I was a baby anyway,' she completed tersely. 'Why are you asking? And how do you even know that I *have* a father living?'

'I had your background investigated while I was waiting for you to get in touch with me,' Leo confessed with a nonchalance that astounded her.

An angry flush illuminated her cheeks. 'You did…*what*? You had me investigated? What gave you the right to go snooping into my background?' Grace launched at him in a sudden fury.

'I needed to know who you were and where you were from…in case you were pregnant,' Leo responded levelly. 'It's standard business practice to check out people before you deal with them.'

'But I *wasn't* business and my life is private!' Grace snapped back at him, outraged by his invasion of her privacy. 'You had no right to pry!'

'I may not have had an official right but I did have good reason to want to know exactly who Grace Donovan and her family were,' Leo retorted unapologetically. 'But to return to my original question—when I found out about your father, it wasn't clear whether or not you had had any recent contact with him.'

Still furious with him, Grace clamped her lips into a tight line of control. 'No, none and I don't want any either!'

His stunning dark golden eyes narrowed in apparent surprise. 'That seems a bit harsh in the circumstances.'

'He let my mother down badly and I'm quite sure he could have traced me years ago if he'd had any real interest in finding me,' Grace declared thinly.

'Only that would have been a considerable challenge for him when your mother had already taken him to court for harassment, had threatened to accuse him of assault and then changed her name to shake him off.'

Sheer rage roared up through Grace's rigid body like a forest fire running out of control. It convulsed her throat muscles, clenched her hands into fists and burned in her chest like the worst ever heartburn. She didn't know what Leo was talking about; she truly didn't have a clue! Wasn't that the ultimate humiliation? How could it ever be right that Leo should know more about her past than *she* did? Harassment? Assault? Court cases?

Reading her shuttered and mutinous face and the pale sea-green eyes blazing at him, Leo returned to the desk and extracted a slim file from the drawer, which he settled on the desk top. 'The investigation. Take it if you want it.'

Trembling with reaction, Grace studiously averted her eyes from the file, too proud to reach for it.

'I didn't intend to upset you, Grace. But naturally, I assumed that nothing in that file would come as a surprise to you…you were eleven years old when you lost your mother.'

Having Leo study her in that cool, even-tempered manner when she herself was so shaken up simply made Grace want to thump him hard. 'You really do have no finer feelings, do you? You suddenly drag up my father and reveal that you know more about him than I do? Didn't it occur to you that that was inexcusably thoughtless and cruel?' she condemned with angry spirit.

'I didn't realise that it would still be such a sensitive subject for you. But you're right—I should've done. I'm not particularly keen to discuss my own background,' Leo conceded with a wry twist of his sensual mouth.

'I have to go. I have an appointment to see my tutor in an hour,' Grace fielded, spinning on her heel and walking fast out of the room before she exposed herself any more.

Leo lifted the investigation file and then slapped it back down hard on the desk in frustration. He had upset her and he hadn't intended to do that. Grace was sensitive. Grace had hang-ups about her past. But didn't he as well? And since when had he worried about such delicate details? Or reacted personally to someone else's distress? The answer to that last question came back and chilled Leo to the marrow: not since he was a child struggling to comfort his distraught mother. Any desire to follow Grace and reason with her faded fast on that note.

Still struggling to master her powerful emotions, Grace leant back against the wall in the lift. What was it about Leo Zikos that brought her inner aggression out? The very first night she had met Leo she had resolved to be herself rather than act like the quieter, more malleable Grace she had learned to be to fit in with her uncle's family. That version of Grace had never freely expressed herself or lost her temper and had certainly never shouted at anyone. So, what was happening to her now? She was unnerved by her own behaviour and by the sheer strength of the emotions taking her by storm. It was almost as though that one night of truly being herself with Leo had destroyed any hope of her either controlling or hiding her emotions again for ever. Suddenly she was feeling all sorts of things she didn't *want* to feel.

Hell roast Leo for his interference, she thought in a simmering tempest of resentment. He had made her curious, made her burn to know what *he* knew about the father she barely remembered and that infuriated her when she had always contrived to keep her curiosity about her father at a manageable, unthreatening level. Now all of a sudden she was desperate to know everything there was to know. But that was yet another betrayal of her self-control, in short a weakness, and she refused to give way to it. After all, she knew everything she needed to know about her father. Those bare facts could only be interpreted in one way. Her father hadn't cared enough to stay around. That was *all* she needed to know, she told herself impatiently.

She met with her tutor and her decision to take a year out from her studies was accepted. While she negotiated the stairs back down to the busy ground floor of the university building, Grace was thinking resolutely positive thoughts about the seed of life in her womb. She was facing huge changes in her life, but the sacrifices she was making and the adjustments that would follow would all benefit her baby, she told herself soothingly.

Marrying Leo would give Grace the precious gift of time. She would have time to come to terms with the prospect of motherhood and time to enjoy the first precious months of her baby's life without the stress of wondering how she was to survive as a new mother. She would also have Leo's support. Any male that keen to marry her for their baby's sake would be a hands-on father and she very much wanted that male influence in her child's life. She had never forgotten how much she herself had longed for a father as a little girl. In every possible way her life would be more settled when she returned to her studies the following year, she reflected with relief.

But as she went to bed that night her mind was still in turmoil over her personal, private reactions to Leo. Leo, always Leo, who had dominated her thoughts from the first moment she laid eyes on him. How had that happened? Grace had always prided herself on her discipline over her emotions but Leo Zikos had blasted through her defensive barriers like a blazing comet, awakening her to feelings and cravings that she had barely understood before. Was it infatuation? Was it simply sexual attraction? Or did her need to understand him, note his gifts as well as his flaws, indicate a deeper, more dangerous form of attachment? Theirs would be a marriage of convenience, after all, and even Marina had warned Grace not to expect more from Leo than he was already offering her.

But in the dark of the night Grace was facing an unsettling truth: she was beginning to fall in love with Leo, hopelessly, deeply in love with a male who had never uttered a word of interest relating to any connection with her more meaningful than sex. A male, moreover, who had virtually blackmailed her into marrying him and who, while declaring respect for fidelity, had still been rampantly unfaithful to his fiancée.

CHAPTER EIGHT

'I CAN'T HELP being curious to know what you know about my father,' Grace admitted stiffly to her uncle on the drive to the register office.

Declan Donovan studied his niece in surprise. 'Virtually nothing, I'm afraid. Your mother refused to talk about him. Initially she said she was getting married but when that failed to transpire Keira had a huge row with our parents and cut us all off. I think she felt she'd lost face with everybody and it hurt her pride.'

'So, you never met him?'

'No, they had a bad break-up and after that we lost track of your mother for years.' The older man shook his head with unhidden regret. 'Keira was a troubled woman, Grace. I never understood her. Luckily she still had my address in her personal effects when she died, so the social worker was able to get in touch with me to tell me about you.'

Grace flushed and looked away, wishing she had asked that same question years sooner. But she had been too proud to ask about the father who had deserted her and her mother. 'It's not important,' she said with forced casualness.

'It's only natural that you would be thinking of your parents on your wedding day,' her uncle completed gruffly and patted her hand.

Leo stared as Grace entered the room and he wasn't the only one. Their few guests copied him, their expressions ranging from admiration to awe and disbelief. Anatole, however, dealt his son an appreciative nod as if the stunning appearance of his son's bride had set the seal on his approval. But then Anatole, Leo acknowledged wryly, had never wanted his son to marry Marina and had instead talked a lot of nonsense about Leo needing to seek a soul mate rather than a practical life partner.

Her wedding dress was the colour of bronze with a metallic gleam, a long simple column that flattered Grace's curves and small stature. In her vibrant hair, which was swept up to show off her slim white throat, she wore only a tawny-coloured exotic hothouse bloom. The pulse beating at Leo's groin flared into disturbing activity, lust flaring when he least welcomed it. A primal surge of desire assailed him as her pale sea-glass eyes collided anxiously with his. She looked incredibly sexy and disturbingly vulnerable.

'Money definitely talks, doesn't it?' Grace's cousin, Jenna, remarked sourly. 'That dress transforms you. It's not very bridal though.'

Grace pasted a smile to her tense lips, determined not to react. It had not escaped her attention that her aunt and her cousin resented the reality that Grace was becoming the wife of a very wealthy man. In any case, Grace's attention had already strayed to Leo, tall and dark and devastatingly handsome in a dark designer suit. Her heart hammered, her tummy flipped. She sucked in her breath, striving to stay calm as he strode across the room, his irresistible smile slashing his beautiful shapely mouth.

'You look stunning,' Leo told her with a dark deep husky edge to his resonant drawl that sent a responsive shiver travelling down her spinal cord. 'Let me introduce you to my father, Anatole.'

'And your brother, Bastien,' the older man slotted in hurriedly as a tall dark male with coldly amused dark eyes strolled up and disconcerted Grace by leaning down to kiss her on both cheeks Continental fashion.

'Enough, Bastien!' Leo grated, startling Grace with that eruption even more.

'Was I trespassing?' Bastien quipped, devilment dancing in his mocking gaze. 'Leo never *did* like to share his toys.'

Leo planted an impatient hand to Grace's spine and spun her away from the other man. 'Some day soon I'll knock his teeth down his throat!' he swore in a raw undertone.

Upset that Bastien had described her as one of Leo's 'toys', Grace flushed and murmured with quiet good sense, 'Shaking hands would have been a little formal when I'm about to join the family.'

'I only count my father as family.' Angry colour scored Leo's high cheekbones.

In answer to his hostility towards his half-brother, Grace simply said nothing and instead turned back to politely address Leo's father, who had been left hovering in discomfiture while his two sons squared up to each other.

Matt approached her almost shyly. 'I hardly recognised you,' he admitted, and they talked about her decision to take a year out until it was time to go into the room next door for the ceremony.

During the ceremony, Grace focused on the handsome flower arrangement on the table while listening carefully to the words. She would have preferred a church service but would not have dreamt of telling Leo that. He slid a ring onto her finger but he had not given her one to return the favour with and there was a small embarrassing pause as the registrar allowed them time to complete what was usually an exchange of rings.

Clearly, Leo wouldn't be wearing a ring, announcing to the world that he was 'taken', Grace reflected ruefully, wondering why that small detail should make her feel so insecure. Many men didn't like wearing rings, she reminded herself.

A light meal was served to the wedding party at an exclusive hotel. Grace glimpsed her reflection in one of the many gilded wall mirrors in the private function room and barely recognised the refined image of the woman clad in the sleek bronze sheath. At the beauty salon the previous day every part of her had been primped and polished and waxed and trimmed, all her rough edges smoothed away. She had seen Della and Jenna's frowning surprise at her new image and she knew she no longer looked incongruous by Leo's side. The cringeworthy fear that her lack of grooming could embarrass Leo had made Grace tolerate the various treatments and she accepted the need to at least *try* to fit into Leo's world as best she could. Grace had always believed that if something was worth doing, it was worth doing well and that was the outlook she intended to embrace in her role as Leo's wife.

'If we're leaving soon I should get changed,' Grace whispered after she had drifted once round the small dance floor in the circle of Leo's arms, every inch of her treacherous body humming at the hard stirring contact with his.

'There's no need for you to change. We should head to the airport now,' Leo told her calmly. 'I'm determined to be the one to take that dress off you, *meli mou*.'

Ready colour warmed Grace's cheeks and within minutes they were walking out to a waiting limousine, having thanked their guests for sharing their day. Travelling with Leo was, she discovered, very different from going on a package holiday trip. There were no queues to slow them down. They were rushed through the airport and waited for the flight call in a private lounge where they were served with refreshments.

'You still haven't told me where we're going,' Grace reminded him.

'Italy…I have a house there. It's very private,' Leo murmured huskily, running a finger across the tender skin of her inner wrist where a blue vein pulsed below her fine white skin, sending a current of awareness snaking through her veins. 'Perfect for a honeymoon.'

They boarded Leo's private jet. The cabin crew greeted her. Grace studied the opulent leather seating and stylish fixtures with wide eyes before she took a seat. She glanced down at the ring gleaming on her wedding finger and breathed in deep and slow. She was Leo's wife now but *only* because she was pregnant, she reminded herself staunchly as the jet took off. It didn't do to forget that salient fact.

A moment later, she was very much taken by surprise when Leo settled the file about her background down on the table in front of her. 'I'm sorry my investigation into your background distressed you but you should know what's in it and I'd like to get it out of the way now.'

Grace paled, tense as a bowstring. She had planned to work up the courage to ask him for the file and she was relieved he had not pushed her to that point. Flipping it open, she began to read. It very quickly became clear that when she was a child she had only been told *one* side of her parents' story—her mother's. And her father's side of the story was strikingly different.

'Were you aware that your mother was an addict?' Leo asked curiously.

'Yes, of course, but I was told to never mention it again once I moved in with my uncle and aunt. They were ashamed of it,' Grace confided ruefully. 'Mum got into drugs when I was a baby but I didn't know that she'd gone into rehab before I was a year old.'

'Your father got her onto a drug rehabilitation programme but it didn't work.'

No, indeed it hadn't, Grace recalled, her disturbing memories of her late mother including many of her lying comatose or doing inappropriate things because she was out of her head on drugs.

'It must've been challenging for him as a doctor to live with an addict, who was the mother of his child.'

'Yes, and of course he inevitably met someone more suitable, another doctor he worked with, and deserted us.'

'But he did take your mother to court first in an effort to gain custody of you…'

That fact was news to Grace. The story she had grown up with had ended with her father Tony's departure from their lives and his marriage to another woman. Now she bent her head over the file and learned that her father had failed to win custody of her from her mother because Keira Donovan had impressed her social worker with her apparent desire to turn her life around. Although her father had been granted access visits to his daughter, there had been continual cancellations and arguments, which had prevented his visits from taking place. By that stage her father had got married and Grace reckoned that her mother's bitterness over that reality would have known no bounds. In an obvious effort to stop the visits, Keira had accused Grace's father of assault and that accusation had plunged Tony into a damaging slew of investigations by the police, the social services and even the General Medical Council. During that period Keira had disappeared and changed her name to ensure that she couldn't be tracked down.

Having failed to trace Keira and their daughter, her father had eventually given up the search. By then he had become a father for the second time and had had a new family to focus on.

'Your mother took you to live in a commune in Wales,' Leo remarked. 'What was that like for you?'

'Ironically it was better than living alone with my mother,' Grace admitted a shade guiltily. 'There were other people around to look out for me and make sure I went to school and had regular meals.'

'You had it tough.'

'I wish my father had found me. I wish he hadn't stopped looking but he was probably afraid that Mum would make more allegations against him and that that might wreck his career.' Grace sighed as she finished reading up to the point where her uncle and aunt had given her a home after her mother's death from an overdose. 'I can't really blame him. Mum was incredibly difficult. She hated him with a passion and she was very bitter.'

'And how do you feel about your father now?' Leo asked levelly.

'That he probably did the best he could and obviously he didn't deliberately abandon me. At least you were lucky enough to have both your parents growing up,' Grace reminded him, closing the file and replacing it on the table with finality. Yet a little burst of warmth had touched the cold, hollow place in her heart where her belief in her father's lack of interest had lodged in childhood. It was good to know that he had cared enough to fight for her even though he had ultimately lost out. For the first time ever, she wondered if she should try and contact her father.

Leo's expressive mouth quirked in receipt of her innocent comment. 'Having both parents never felt lucky to me. Anatole married my mother, who was a very spoiled Greek heiress, primarily for her money.'

Grace gazed back at him in shock. 'That's an awful thing to accuse your father of!'

'But regretfully true. Although he married my mother he was actually in love with a waitress called Athene. He set Athene up as a mistress and she became pregnant with Bastien only a few months after my mother conceived me,' he confided grimly. 'Eventually my mother found out that she wasn't the only woman in her husband's life. I must've been about six by then. I still remember her screaming, sobbing and throwing things and the drama went on for days. Anatole duly promised to give up Athene and we lived in peace for a while. But of course Anatole was lying and the truth came out again. That same destructive pattern just kept on repeating and repeating—'

'That must've been devastating for your mother. She must've really loved your father to keep on forgiving him.'

'But *he* loved Athene and obviously Bastien was almost the same age as I was, so in a sense Anatole had *two* families. It was a hideous triangle.' His lean dark features were bleak. 'Anatole couldn't walk away from Athene and my mother refused to let him go. Once when he tried to leave her she took sleeping pills and that scared the life out of him.'

'Of course it did,' Grace said with a shiver.

'When I was thirteen, Athene died in a car crash and Bastien came to live with us. My mother was so relieved that her rival was dead that she agreed to the arrangement. Naturally, Bastien and I didn't hit it off,' Leo said drily, his lean, darkly handsome features grim. 'However, the volatile nature of my parents' marriage convinced me that I didn't want an atom of that obsessive passion in my own marriage…'

Grace sipped at her soft drink and searched his lean, strong face, recognising the gravity etched there. 'Meaning?'

'I have never wanted any part of the possessiveness, the jealousy, the arguments or the overly high expectations that most married couples have of each other.'

'That's the down side of attachment. Love is the upside,' Grace told him gently.

'Not for me, it isn't,' Leo countered with cool conviction. 'I'm not looking for love in our marriage, Grace.'

In spite of the sinking sensation in her stomach, Grace threw him a brilliant smile. 'Neither am I, Leo, but I *will* expect you to love our child.'

'That's a different kind of love,' he declared.

'A less selfish love certainly,' she conceded, wanting to ask him about his relationship with Marina and biting her lip to restrain herself while she was uncertain of her ground. 'You forgave your father for his mistakes, didn't you?'

'He's a good-hearted man but weak at the core. He dug himself into a hole and he couldn't get out of it. He didn't want to hurt anyone by making a choice and the result was that he hurt *all* of us.'

Her lashes dipped over her sea-glass eyes,

which were clear as jade in the light filling the cabin. 'If you feel so strongly about your father's infidelity, how could you cheat on Marina?'

'But I didn't...*cheat* on her,' Leo contradicted with a flare of distaste in the brilliant dark eyes narrowed below the lush canopy of his lashes. 'Marina and I got engaged and then agreed to go our separate ways until we got married.'

Her lashes fluttered up in disbelief. 'That's weird.'

'Why? Neither of us was in a hurry to marry and we weren't lovers either, so it wasn't the unsavoury agreement you are obviously imagining,' Leo derided.

We weren't lovers. That phrase repeated inside Grace's brain and stunned her. 'You mean, you and Marina...er...*never*—?'

'Never, but that is confidential.'

Grace was shocked into silence, recalling Marina's comment about Leo's indifference and finally understanding its source. That Leo had been content to stand back and allow Marina to do as she liked during their engagement spoke volumes about the chilling level of his detachment and it was hardly surprising that the brunette had ultimately decided that she would be happier with another man. And Marina's statement that Leo was bad for her ego? Oh, yes, Grace finally understood that and the significant part it might well play in her own future. Would Leo be so detached with her that he froze her out too?

The jet landed in Tuscany and they transferred into a helicopter for the last leg of their journey. By that stage Grace was fed up bundling her long dress round her legs to cope with steps and looking forward to being free of its confines, not to mention her perilously high heels. She stole a tentative glance at Leo's hard bronzed profile, recalling his declared intention to remove her dress. Steamy warmth engulfed her treacherous body, anticipation as potent as an electrical storm at its core. But then desire shimmied like intoxicating alcohol through her veins when Leo was close. A heady combination of memory and the physical craving he evoked put her on edge, mortified by her weakness and ill at ease with her own physical reactions.

Leo lifted her out of the helicopter when they landed and she straightened to look in wonder at the building a hundred yards from them. 'It's a castle!'

'Yes, but a small one. Built by a wealthy eccentric in the nineteen twenties and bought by my mother. She owned a lot of property round the world. I turned the most promising into businesses and sold the rest,' he volunteered, walking her towards the curiously elegant castle fashioned of cream-coloured stone and set in the midst of beautiful gardens. 'At one time I planned to turn the castle into a small exclusive hotel but once I had renovated it I decided to keep it as a bolt-hole.'

'It's hot for this time of year,' Grace remarked in pleasant surprise, moving into the cool shadow of the tree-lined stone path that led to the castle entrance. Back in London late summer was fading into evenings with steadily dropping temperatures while here in Tuscany the roses were still blooming and the bite of autumn's approach had yet to register.

A cheerful housekeeper chattering in Italian met them on the doorstep. Leo introduced her as Josefina and responded smoothly in the same language before escorting Grace across the highly polished floor tiles in the hall and up the stone staircase. A selection of doors led off the wide landing but Leo headed straight for the set of double doors in the centre and into a massive bedroom with a turret at either corner.

'Wow,' she whispered, pulling away from him to explore the turrets, finding a bathroom in one and a fully furnished dressing room in the other.

An ebony brow lifted, Leo watched in amusement, enjoying the expressions crossing her mobile face while their cases were being stashed behind them. 'You like?'

'I *love*,' Grace confided, kicking off the high heels, which pinched. She brushed the petal of an exquisite white lily in a dramatic floral arrangement, trailed an admiring finger along the gleaming wooden surface of an antique chest of drawers and studied the big bed with its snowy white linen and ice-blue silky throw. 'It's so romantic.'

'I don't do romance,' he reminded her, unbuttoning his shirt, having long since discarded his jacket and tie.

'Bite the bullet, Leo,' Grace advised in amusement. 'This is a very romantic setting.'

Leo stiffened, but looking away from Grace at that moment wasn't an option; she looked so impossibly appealing. She had taken her hair down during the flight and the brilliantly colourful strands tumbled luxuriantly round her slim shoulders, glinting like her metallic dress in the sunlight coming through the windows. He moved forward, stepped behind her and ran down her zip, peeling the fabric back slowly from her shoulders while planting a kiss on the pale flesh he exposed.

Grace held her breath, watching their reflections merge in a tall mirror with the faint blurry quality of antique glass. As he bent over her, the brush of his lips made her shiver. His hair was so black against hers, his hand so dark against her white shoulder. The dress slid down her arms and then dropped in a pool at her feet.

'My turn to say wow,' Leo growled, flipping her round to take in the full effect of her curves sheathed in a dainty white balcony bra and knickers teamed with lace hold-up stockings. 'I like…I *love*.'

'Th-thought you would,' Grace stammered, her face burning with colour because standing in front of him clad in provocative lingerie filled her with stupid self-consciousness.

'I'm very easy to please,' Leo husked, tipping her breasts gently free of the silk to massage her pointed pink nipples between finger and thumb, lowering a hand to slide a fingertip beneath the edge of her panties and probe the wet heat she would have hidden from him.

An arrow of stark hunger shot through Grace and she gasped, wanting, needing, pierced by so many sensations at once she couldn't vocalise or think. He crushed her parted lips below his, nibbling and teasing with erotic expertise, and then lifted his head again.

'I want you so much I'm burning with it,' Leo breathed, dropping to his knees to tug down her knickers and spread her thighs. 'And I want you to burn along with me, *hara mou*.'

Grace shivered in sensual shock as he closed his mouth to the most sensitive spot on her entire body. She couldn't believe she was standing there, letting him… All too quickly her knees shook with weakness as she drowned in the intoxicating flood of pleasure he was wrenching from her. Little breathy cries parted her lips, sounds punctuated by a low keening moan. Suddenly it was more than she could bear and it took his hands curving to her hips to keep her upright as the excitement pent up inside her surged high and took her with it in an orgasm that almost tipped her off her feet.

But no, that was Leo's doing as he caught her weak body up into his arms and pinned her down on the bed, leaning over her as he yanked off his clothes with an impatience she could feel in every fibre of her still-humming body.

'Seems to me you're always promising to do this slowly,' Grace whispered.

'I'm not going to deliver slow tonight either,' Leo warned, coming down to her again naked and urgently aroused. 'I'm too damned excited.'

It thrilled Grace that she had the power to unleash such impatience in him. She felt the push of him against her tender flesh and lifted her legs to lock her thighs round his lean hips in welcome, the wanting building again like some monster she couldn't sate because, even when she was fresh from a mind-blowing climax, Leo could somehow make her want him again. Her heart was hammering, her body slick with perspiration and every skin cell was on fire for him so that when he thrust deep into her, she cried out with the hot pleasure of that powerful invasion. He withdrew and sank into her again, choosing a potent rhythm that sent heat pulsing through her pelvis as her greedy body began to strain and burn and reach for the heights again.

'Oh, please, don't stop!' she heard herself gasp in anguished excitement.

She was soaring by then, her body jerking and convulsing with the sheer raw intensity of the pleasure washing over her. Bliss enclosed her like a warm soft cocoon when it was over but a little buzzer also went off in her head, reminding her of how Leo pulled away from intimacy in the aftermath of sex. In a sudden movement, Grace dislodged him and snaked out of the bed to head straight for the bathroom. The very knowledge that she wanted to hug him and stay close had sent her into swift retreat for fear of what she might reveal. There was no room for such sentimental behaviour within the narrow limits Leo had set for their marriage.

A few minutes later, Leo stepped into the spacious wet room to join her. 'What was that all about?' he asked.

'What was *what* all about?'

'You pushed me away,' he reminded her, angry dark eyes spelling out how he had reacted to her conduct.

'That's what you've always done with me afterwards,' Grace pointed out innocently. 'Shouldn't I have done that?'

Leo knew when he was being played, but then he had also never been on the receiving end of such a careless dismissal before. It had stung, it had felt ridiculously like rejection, he reasoned in confusion at his own thoughts. Before he could think any more, he reacted on instinct and closed Grace's dripping body into his arms below the falling spray.

'Things change. We're married now. I think we can afford to be a little more affectionate,' he declared in a rasping undertone, tugging her even closer.

Grace hid a smile against a broad muscular shoulder. He wasn't an irredeemable rat, she decided ruefully. Damaged by his parents' toxic marriage, he had avoided the softer emotions all his life to date. But he could learn by example, yes, and he was one very fast learner, Grace conceded as the embrace became an unashamed hug.

A couple of hours later, they lay naked in a tangle of fur throws in front of the gas-fired logs in the massive fireplace in the main drawing room. As night fell they had become hungry and had raided the fridge to savour the delicacies prepared by Josefina, the housekeeper, who had gone home hours earlier.

'I thought pregnant women suffered a lot from nausea,' Leo said abruptly. 'But you still have a good appetite.'

'I haven't felt sick once,' Grace admitted. 'A little dizzy a couple of times but that's all.'

'I've signed you up to see one of the local doctors while we're here.'

'That's unnecessary this early in my pregnancy.'

Leo dealt her a warning glance. 'Humour me. I have a very strong need to know that I'm looking after you properly.'

But Grace was worried that if she gave an inch, Leo would take a mile. She wondered if he had taken the same managing, controlling attitude to Marina and asked.

Leo rested back thoughtfully on his hands, the hard muscular lines of his chest and stomach flexing taut and drawing her involuntary gaze. 'I never felt the need to interfere…offer advice occasionally, yes, veto or demand, no. You're different.'

'How am I different?' Grace asked baldly.

'You're pregnant,' Leo pointed out, disappointing her with that comeback.

'So, if I'm allowed to ask one awkward question…exactly why *did* you want to marry Marina?'

'Because I thought she was perfect…'

Grace froze, the colour leaching from beneath her fair skin.

'Of course, nobody is perfect,' Leo continued wryly. 'But I did believe Marina was as near to the ideal as I could get because we had so much in common and were close friends.'

Never ask a question if you aren't tough enough to accept the answer and live with it, Grace told herself wretchedly. How on earth could she compete with his ideal of the perfect wife? Most especially when that ideal woman was still walking around? Was it possible that Leo felt more for Marina than he had ever appreciated? And that losing her might make him finally realise it? Not a productive thought train, Grace scolded herself, and she suppressed her crushing sense of insecurity with every fibre of willpower that she possessed.

'So, why don't you want these blood tests the doctor has recommended?' Leo demanded impatiently.

Grace wrinkled her nose. 'Because there's nothing wrong with me.'

'But the doctor—'

'Dr Silvano is nice but he is a little old-fashioned, Leo. Why should he wonder if there's something wrong with my hormone levels just because I'm not feeling sick all the time?' Grace prompted impatiently. 'A lot of women get morning sickness but there are a lucky few who *don't* and I don't plan to start fussing over myself and worrying without good reason. He's one of those doctors who prefer to treat pregnancy as an illness and I don't agree with that.'

Leo surveyed her with unhidden annoyance. Grace went pink and looked across the cobbled square to the playground where small children were running and shouting. In a few years she would have a child of around that age, she ruminated fondly, wishing Leo would not make her pregnancy so much *his* business. Yet how could she fault a man for caring about her well-being?

'I'll go back first thing tomorrow for the tests,' Grace surrendered with a grimace. 'Will that make you happy?'

The tightness of his superb bone structure eased and the hint of a smile softened the hard line of his sculpted mouth. They had been in Italy for four incredible weeks and even when Leo annoyed her, Grace still never got tired of simply looking at him, admiring the proud flare of his nose, the downward frown of his brows when anything annoyed him, the pure silk ebony luxuriance of his lashes when he looked down at her with eyes of pure gold in bed.

'Yes, that will make me happy,' Leo told her without apology and pulled out his phone to immediately book the appointment.

Grace sipped her bottled water, reflecting that Leo had taught her a master class in the art of compromise and negotiation. His forceful personality and strong views made occasional clashes between them inevitable. He was much deeper and more of a thinker than he liked to show. Clever, shrewd and over-protective as he was, he was also wonderfully entertaining and her every fantasy in bed. He was willing to make an effort as well. Since their wedding night there had been no further flights from intimacy post-climax. She wouldn't let herself think negative thoughts around him, wouldn't let herself dwell on the awareness that she loved him and he did not love her. Unlike him, she wasn't expecting the perfect marital partner.

And in any case, Leo might say that he didn't do romance but it was remarkable how often their outings were drenched in romantic views, surroundings and meals. He had taken her to see a candlelit religious procession in the streets of Lucca one evening and topped it off with dinner in a rooftop restaurant with the stars shimmering far above them. They had enjoyed a picnic below the ancient chestnut trees that overlooked the vineyards in the valley. With no road noise, no people around and virtually nothing in view to remind them of the twentieth century, it had been timeless and peaceful and she had dozed off, probably because she had eaten far too much from Josefina's fantastic picnic dishes. There had been sightseeing trips and scenic drives and a couple of casual dinner engagements with friends Leo had, who lived locally.

And then there were the shopping trips and the gifts. Grace tilted her chin, green eyes reflective as she glanced at the gold watch on her wrist and thought about the pearls in her ears and at her throat, not to mention the gorgeous handbag she had foolishly admired in a shop window. Leo was very generous and his giving wasn't soulless or showing off. If he noticed she lacked something like jewellery he provided it without fanfare and so smoothly it was impossible to politely refuse. No, she couldn't fault his intellect, his company, his generosity or the high-voltage excitement of his sexuality.

Furthermore after a month of living with Leo round the clock she could no longer credit the belief that he had blackmailed her into marrying him.

'When you threatened my uncle and aunt's careers, you were bluffing, weren't you?' Grace condemned very drily.

Leo rocked back in his chair, lashes low over gleaming dark eyes. 'I was wondering how long it would take you to work that out.'

Temper hurtled through Grace like a rejuvenating blast of oxygen. 'You mean you wouldn't have done it?'

'Of course I wouldn't have done it. I'm not an unjust man. Your uncle gave you a home when you needed one and I respect him for that because I doubt very much that he received much support from your aunt.' Leo studied her. 'But from certain things you have let slip quite without meaning to, I think your aunt should be burnt at the stake as a witch…and possibly your cousin with her.'

That cool rundown of her upbringing snuffed out Grace's annoyance as though it had never been and provoked an involuntary laugh from her lips. 'Oh…dear.'

'But in one sense you have done me a favour. Your position in your uncle's family closely resembled Bastien's when my half-brother and I were children and that has enabled me to see that Bastien was often excluded, set apart from my parents and I by his birth and parentage and made to feel like an outsider,' he imparted grimly. 'It was wrong when that was done to you and it must follow that it was equally wrong when it was done to him.'

Grace nodded, impressed by that deduction and his willingness to admit fault on that score. The level of animosity between Leo and his brother had disconcerted her. She suspected they never met without one trying to score points off the other.

'Sadly, that reality won't make me *like* Bastien but it is why I was ready to allow you to believe that I would blackmail you into marriage. I was prepared to use any weapon you put within my reach,' Leo confessed wryly. 'I could not bear our child to experience the isolation which you and Bastien suffered as children. I don't ever want a child of mine to feel like an outsider. And if you and I hadn't married that is what he or she would have ultimately been.'

'So, I'm supposed to forgive the blackmail threats because your goal was the greater good?' Grace fielded very drily although grudging amusement was tugging at her lips. 'With that kind of reasoning you could excuse murder, Leo.'

A wolfish grin slashed Leo's darkly handsome face. 'But you *like* being married to me?'

Grace rested her chin down on the heel of her hand and gave him an enquiring look. 'And why do you assume that?'

'You sing in the shower, you smile at me a lot...you even jump me in bed occasionally,' Leo husked soft and low, dark golden eyes pure burnished gold with wicked amusement and that innate bold assurance that she found so outrageously compelling.

Grace didn't quite know how to react to that unexpectedly personal list of her mistakes. For smiling at him all the time was a dead giveaway of the kind of feelings he didn't want her to have and she didn't want to reveal. But it was a challenge to hide the simple truth that he made her happy, indeed happier than anyone had ever made her feel in her entire life. Because while he might not love her, he did *care* and he seemed to find her irresistible. Did she really need more than that from him? All that lovey-dovey stuff and wedding rings proudly worn on male fingers would really just be the icing on the cake, she reasoned: lovely to have but not strictly necessary.

'You won't be getting jumped tonight,' she warned him, her lovely face flushed and self-conscious.

And Leo laughed uproariously as he so often

did with Grace, who teased him and came back at him verbally in a way no other woman ever had and who was nothing short of dirty dynamite in his bed. Oh, no, Leo had no complaints on the marriage front. In fact, Leo was delighted with his bride.

He walked her back to the car and noticed a guy on a motorbike twisting his head rather dangerously to get a second look at the figure Grace cut in a pale pink cami top that showed rather more cleavage than Leo liked and a clinging white skirt that enhanced her curvy behind and show-stopping legs. His mouth flattened while he wondered when Grace would start *looking* more pregnant and less curvy and sexy. He could hardly wait for the day. It offended him when other men studied his wife with lascivious intent.

Grace was glad of the breeze that cooled her as they walked into the castle because she was feeling uncomfortably warm. 'I need a shower,' she sighed, starting up the stairs.

'Me too,' Leo husked with a roughened edge to his dark deep drawl.

Grace was moving towards the bathroom when Leo spoke again and in a sudden tone of urgency. 'Grace…your skirt…you're *bleeding*!'

CHAPTER NINE

COLD SHOCK AND dismay filled Grace as she looked down at herself. In the bathroom she frantically peeled off her clothes.

'You can't have a shower now...you should lie down!' Leo tried to remonstrate with her.

'Don't be silly,' Grace argued shakily. 'If I'm having a miscarriage there's nothing anyone can do to stop it.'

Leo stepped out of the bathroom to call Dr Silvano and then went back in, battling an angry, aggressive urge to snatch Grace bodily out of the shower and force her to lie down but very much afraid that coming over all caveman would only upset her more. He tried to wrap a huge towel round her when she came out, hovering even when she shouted at him to leave her alone. Grace rebelled by stepping back out of view to take care of necessities but he was still waiting with the towel when she emerged again.

'You're so cold,' he groaned.

'Shock,' she said, teeth chattering while she struggled to make herself face what felt like an impossible challenge and slid her arms into a towelling robe. 'You know one in four pregnancies end in miscarriage during the first trimester and I'm only eight weeks and a bit along...'

'Hush,' Leo incised, bundling her up into his arms and carrying her over to the bed before rattling through drawers in search of the nightdress she requested. 'Are you in a lot of pain?'

She winced. 'None...whatsoever.'

'You'll still have to go into hospital. *Diavelos*...I should've taken you straight there!' Leo breathed, pacing the floor at the end of the bed, rigid with tension and regret.

'No hospital, Leo. I think I'd freak out on a gynae ward surrounded by pregnant women and newborns.'

'You'd be in a private room and don't be so

pessimistic,' Leo censured. 'It may not be what you fear.'

Grace said nothing. She lay as still as an upturned statue staring up at the ceiling. Crazy thoughts tormented her. Was this to be her punishment for thinking that she could give her baby up for adoption? Was this her punishment for not properly valuing the gift she had been given? It seemed that Dr Silvano had been right when he'd expressed the opinion that a mother-to-be suffering from nausea and sore breasts could indicate a more stable pregnancy. Her eyes prickled. It was inconceivable to her that only an hour earlier she and Leo had been laughing and carefree, utterly unaware of what lay ahead.

She was moved from the limo into the small hospital in a wheelchair and taken to a small side ward. Somewhere in the background she could hear Leo talking in low-pitched urgent Italian and thought numbly of how useful his gift with languages could be. A few minutes later she was moved yet again and this time she was transferred to a room where there were no other patients. Leo helped her into bed and the fraught silence between them worked on Grace's nerves until a radiographer entered with a portable scanner. Grace lay still while the gelled probe moved back and forth over her tummy, her attention locked to the small screen, her hopes and dreams slowly dying as what she prayed for failed to appear. The operator excused herself and reappeared some minutes later with a doctor, who spoke English. He broke the news that the machine had failed to detect the baby's heartbeat but that the procedure would be repeated the following day to ensure that there was no mistake.

'I don't see why we should wait twenty-four hours to get a confirmation.' Leo breathed harshly, his bone structure rigid below his bronzed skin.

'It's standard procedure to wait twenty-four hours and check again,' Grace chipped in.

'I'll organise an airlift to a city hospital, somewhere with the latest equipment,' he began.

The doctor said that it would not be a good

idea to move Grace again and that air travel at such an early stage of her pregnancy only heightened the likelihood of miscarriage.

'I'm not going anywhere,' Grace declared, turning her face into the wall because she could not bear to continue looking at Leo.

It was over. Why was he making everything more difficult by fighting the obvious conclusion? Most probably she had miscarried and everyone in the room with the exception of Leo could accept that. A second check tomorrow was very probably only a routine precaution.

But then she was not cut from the same cloth as her husband, she acknowledged heavily. Leo was rich and powerful and accustomed to his wealth changing negatives into positives but sadly there was no way to do that in the current situation. Her baby had died without ever learning what it would be like to live. A great swell of anguish mushroomed up through Grace and a choked sob escaped her as she gasped for breath and control.

Leo sat down on the side of the bed and gripped

her clenched fingers. 'We'll get through this,' he rasped, his eyes burning and pinned to her pale, pinched profile as he flailed around mentally striving to come up with words of comfort.

'It just wasn't meant to be,' Grace said with flat conviction.

'Some day there'll be…another chance,' Leo completed tightly.

'Not for us.'

Leo ignored that assurance. He wasn't about to get into an argument. Grace was devastated, probably barely aware of what she was saying and Leo, struggling to master the tightness in his chest and the yawning hollow opening up inside him, was realising that he was devastated too, much more devastated than he had ever expected to be in such circumstances. 'Let's not be pessimistic. Tomorrow…'

'It will only hurt me more to hold onto false hope!' Grace snapped back at him, her head flipping, vibrant red hair spilling across the pillows, pale sea-glass eyes distraught and accusing.

Leo's eyes stung, frustration flaring through

his lean, powerful frame because he wanted so badly to fix things and knew that he couldn't. 'It was my baby too,' he murmured in a roughened undertone.

'I know…that's *all* you ever cared about. Believe me, I don't need reminding,' Grace framed jerkily, turning away again to present him with her slender back.

Leo paled and sprang off the bed to head for the chair in the corner. 'Try to get some sleep. I'll stay with you.'

Grace sat up with a sudden start, grief and regret weighing her down to the extent that she felt as if she were drowning in inner turmoil and unhappiness. She pushed the pillows back behind her and studied him in his pale grey exquisitely tailored suit that glimmered like dull silver below the stark hospital lights. His blue-black hair was tousled, his strong jawline rough with dark stubble, his stunning eyes unusually bright with emotion. Of course he was upset; she *knew* he was upset. After all, much as he might wish to be, he *wasn't* a block of unfeeling wood. Unfortunately, Grace had already looked beyond their loss to become painfully aware of exactly what her miscarriage meant to them as a newly married couple.

'There's no point in you staying.'

Predictably, Leo argued. He needed to be with her. That was non-negotiable in his mind. He had to see that she was fed, properly cared for and that if things were to get any worse he was on the spot to provide immediate support. His sense of responsibility was too strong to be denied.

'Why would you stay?' Grace whispered, fighting her desire for his presence, fighting her longing for him to come close again, fighting all those softer feelings with the sure knowledge at that moment that she was doing what *had* to be done. She was facing up to reality, struggling to move forward and step away from the lure of a future that could no longer be hers. How could she feel any other way when that future had been so inextricably linked to their baby?

'You're my wife, *hara mou*. I belong by your side,' Leo countered with fierce conviction.

'You're upset, we're both upset but together we're stronger.'

'Maybe that would've been true had we been in love…but obviously we're not.' Grace closed her restive fingers into a tight ball of self-restraint, her deep sense of hurt tamped down. 'Us…as a couple, that's *over*. Of course it is. How could it be anything else after what's just happened?' she asked shakily, anger at the tumultuous emotions she was crushing arrowing through her trembling frame because with every word she spoke she was going against her own heart.

But how could she do anything else? she asked herself in despair. They had come together for the baby's sake and without the baby there was nothing to keep them together. She had to face that, deal with it, *live* with it whether she liked it or not. She loved him but he did not love her. She was too proud and too fair-minded to cling to him and make him feel that he somehow owed it to her to stay with her.

Leo welded long tanned fingers to the rail at the foot of her bed, every muscle in his lean, powerful body pulling dangerously tight. 'I don't know what you're talking about,' he said in a harsh undertone.

'I'm just saying what needs to be said. You're *free*, Leo.'

Leo lost colour, the exotic slant of his cheekbones pronounced. There was a lurch in the region of his gut as though he had been punched. He didn't want to be free. Naturally he had got used to being married and he was content to stay married and eventually try for another baby. Grace suited him. He didn't know how she did it or why she was so important to him but she matched him in all the ways that mattered. Indeed he had become so accustomed to Grace being around that he could not imagine his life without her. Obviously he was more of a creature of habit and routine than he had ever appreciated because within a short time Grace had become astonishingly necessary to his comfort.

'And what if I don't want to be free?' he grated, soft and low.

'If that's what you *think* you feel right now

you're *lying* to yourself,' Grace told him with astonishing conviction. 'And why are you lying to yourself? Because you feel sorry for me and you think it's your job to look after me. You have a very strong sense of responsibility and that's a noble trait but don't let it blind you to what you really want out of life. And what you really want, Leo, is *not* me.'

Leo wondered why *she* was telling *him* how he felt. Did she really think he was so inadequate that he couldn't work out his own feelings for himself? Annoyance slashed through him and he wanted to express it but he was horrendously aware of the experience she had undergone and that it was his duty not to make the situation worse.

'Our marriage was all about the baby and everything you have ever shared with me related to the baby and the baby's future needs. Without our baby…' Grace framed unsteadily, tears glinting in her over-bright eyes '…we don't have a marriage. We don't even have a relationship. We can get a divorce now.'

'Are you insane?' Leo heard himself snap back at her, all self-discipline vanquished by her use of that bombshell word. *Divorce?* How was he supposed to listen to that in polite and understanding silence?

'I'm looking at a guy who doesn't even wear a wedding ring!' Grace shot at him equally out of the blue and Leo looked down at his bare hand in bewilderment, wondering what wedding rings had to do with anything and whether simply leaving the room would be wiser than remaining.

'You never bothered to ask but I would've liked to get married in a church. But then you never really wanted to be properly married to me, so obviously you didn't bother to ask my preferences. You didn't *choose* me,' Grace condemned heatedly. 'You married me because I was pregnant, so why would we stay together now?' she demanded emotively.

Leo lifted stunned dark golden eyes from the offending hand that lacked a wedding ring and thought how sneaky women could be. She had never mentioned his omission or the church thing. She had never by so much as a hint let him know how she felt about him not wearing a wedding ring and now he was being hung out to dry for a sin he hadn't known he had committed. How fair was that?

'I can buy a wedding ring,' Leo pointed out gruffly.

'That's not the point!' Grace exclaimed in seething frustration because he was not giving her the reaction she had expected: he was not looking guiltily relieved.

'Then why did you mention it? And could we have this conversation at some other time when you're not emotionally overwrought and we're both feeling calmer?' Leo pressed grittily. 'Because right now is not working for me.'

Grace lifted her chin. 'I thought it was better to say it and get it out in the open. I don't want you faking what you don't feel. You felt things for the baby, not for me.'

'That is untrue,' Leo grated, losing patience.

'You're my wife and I made a serious commitment to you.'

'But I don't want your cold sense of commitment…I want love!' Grace flung back at him helplessly.

'I warned you that I couldn't put that on the table,' Leo breathed harshly.

'Oh, you could if you wanted to,' Grace fielded with unmistakeable bitterness. 'But you don't want to. And do you know why? It's not because you had an unhappy childhood, it's because you're an emotional coward.'

His nostrils flared, his eyes kindling like flames. 'Let's not descend to that level.'

'But it's true. You don't get involved because you're scared of getting hurt. Nobody wants to get hurt, Leo, but most of us still *try* to make a relationship that goes further than practicality and convenient sex. You're too busy protecting yourself to even give it a go.' Exhausted by telling him what was wrong with their marriage, Grace fell back against the pillows, drained by emotion. 'Go back to the castle.'

'To start planning our divorce?' Leo challenged darkly.

'It's inevitable now,' she whispered numbly, her heart heavy as lead inside her tight chest. 'There's nothing left to keep us together.'

'If you really want me to leave, I'll leave and come back first thing in the morning,' he bit out grimly, his darkly handsome features bleak with constraint.

'There's no point you coming back for the second scan.' Grace knew she would cry then because, no matter how hard she was striving to be realistic, a little spark of hope still flourished inside her. She would be shattered when she received the confirmation that, yes, she had miscarried and lost their baby and she didn't want Leo to witness that emotional breakdown and start feeling sorry for her again. 'I could handle that better alone. I'll be able to leave the hospital straight after it.'

'To do what? Fly back to London?' Leo demanded bitterly. 'You're in no fit state for that. At the very least you need to spend a couple of weeks recuperating. If it makes you happier, I'll leave and you can have the castle all to yourself. At this moment I feel that getting fully back to work would be a welcome distraction.'

'I didn't want it to be like this, Leo,' Grace muttered wretchedly. 'I know you're upset as well.'

'I'm not upset.' Leo swung round and left the room, walked down the corridor and settled in the waiting room. He wasn't just upset, he was furious. She was his wife and she was shutting him out, dismissing him as a husband as if he were of no account.

Did he really deserve a wife who had such a low opinion of him? Did she think he had been faking it with her for the whole of the past month? Faking the passion, the laughter, the enjoyment? Without warning he badly wanted a drink and he wanted to punch something hard. He leapt upright again and paced. Grace was stubborn and rigid in her views. That wedding-ring jibe? How could she be so petty?

Unfortunately, her prejudice against her father

for the way she had believed he had treated her late mother had ensured that Grace had not had a very high opinion of men even to begin with. And how much had Leo's own behaviour since their first meeting contributed to her continuing distrust? The casual one-night stand? The engagement he had neglected to mention? The blackmail he had used to persuade her to marry him? His conduct had been less than stellar.

But Leo had always had a can-do approach to problems. Grace wanted him to love her? He could lie and tell her he loved her. Was he willing to do *anything* to keep her? Leo winced, shocked by the concept. What had she done to his brain? His brain clearly wasn't working properly. Shock and sorrow had temporarily deranged his wits because for the first time since childhood he felt helpless and almost panicky.

It felt wrong not being with Grace although maybe she genuinely needed time alone to deal with what had happened. He couldn't help wishing she had turned to him, *leant* on him. He spoke to the nurse in charge, asking her to conact him if Grace's condition changed, and then he breathed in deep and fought his reluctance to leave the hospital. Perhaps if Grace slept a while, she would be more normal in the morning, a little less worked up and fatalistic, although it was hard to see how a confirmation of the miscarriage would do anything to improve her outlook.

Leo helped himself to a whiskey in his limousine. He would get stinking drunk and stop agonising over a situation he couldn't fix, he decided despondently. He checked his phone to see if Grace had texted him; she had not. He embarked on a second whiskey while wondering if a wedding ring could really mean that much to a woman and he thought about texting Grace to ask to have that mystery explained. But there was a yawning hole stretching ever wider somewhere inside his chest. He thought about the baby, the baby that wasn't going to be, and his eyes burned and prickled, deep regret engulfing him.

He lifted his phone again, needing to talk to Grace, wanting to share his thoughts with a woman for the first time ever. He'd probably wake her up or upset her by saying the wrong thing, he conceded heavily. And the last thing she needed was a series of drunken maudlin texts asking silly questions. But the phone, the only link he had with the woman he so badly wanted to be with, was a terrible temptation. After a moment's reflection, Leo extracted his SIM card, buzzed down the window and flung his phone out of the car. There, now he couldn't be tempted to do or say anything stupid.

Grace tossed and turned restively in the bed, tears trickling from below her lowered eyelids. She wanted Leo, she wanted him back so badly, but he had never really belonged to her in the way a *real* husband would have done and now she needed to learn not to look for him and not to rely on him. She had to accept that this phase of her life was over. There would not be a baby with Leo. He had been so angry when he'd left her and she knew she had provoked him. He had tried to be there for her and she had rejected him, needing him to see that honesty was now the best policy. Their shotgun marriage no longer had a reason to exist and she had recognised that reality long before he did. Wasn't that better than Leo waking up some day about a year from now and questioning why he was still married to a woman so far removed from his ideal of a wife?

Yet the prospect of life without Leo, life *after* Leo was unbearable to Grace. She couldn't sleep and it was mid-morning before she was taken to be scanned. This time the scanner was a bigger, more complex machine and the doctor was present. Grace lay still, all hope of good news crushed by a wretched sleepless night and an irredeemable tendency to expect only bad things to happen to her. So, when the doctor urged her in heavily accented English to look at the screen, she was reluctant and glanced up, startled to see that the small medical team surrounding her were all smiling.

And they showed her baby's heartbeat and switched on the sound so that she could listen to that racing beat that quickened her own. An intense sense of joyous relief filled her with a wash of powerful emotion and tears flooded her eyes. 'I was so sure I'd lost my baby…'

The obstetrician sat down by her side to enumerate the various reasons why bleeding could occur in early pregnancy, pointing out that her blood loss had already stopped and that her baby's heartbeat was strong and regular.

The minute she got back to her room, Grace snatched up her phone to text Leo, but what on earth was she to say to him? What an idiot she had been! Panicking and distraught at the conviction she had lost their baby, she had flung their marriage on the bonfire of her hopes as well. It would be her own fault if Leo received the news that he was still going to be a father with a new sense of regret because she had blown their relationship apart with all her foolish talk about wanting love. She laboured long over the text she sent him, apologising profusely for the way she had behaved and the things she had said before sharing the fact that she was still pregnant. She was a little surprised that there was no immediate response and rather more disconcerted when a nurse came to tell her that a car had arrived to collect her and she was wheeled out expecting to see Leo and instead saw only his driver and two of his bodyguards. Had she expected Leo to rush hotfoot to the hospital to greet her?

Perhaps that had been a little unrealistic after what she had slung at him the evening before, she conceded wretchedly. She sent him another text, hoping to elicit a response, but it was not until the evening that Leo phoned her and the conversation they shared was brief and stilted. He asked how she was, made no reference to the baby or their marriage and told her that he was in London on business and that he would be away for about a week.

'When you get back, I suppose we'll talk,' Grace said uncomfortably, disappointed that he hadn't once mentioned the baby.

'Great…won't that be something to look forward to?' Leo derided, silencing her altogether.

Had Leo ignored her text because he had decided that there was a lot of truth in what she had said at the hospital? Had he reached the conclusion that the fact they were going to be parents wasn't a good enough reason to stay married to a woman who wasn't his ideal? Was that why he had made no comment? And was the divorce she had suggested what he would be discussing when he reappeared?

Five days later, Grace sat out on the terrace below the twining vines that were slowly colouring to autumnal shades and dropping their leaves. She had thrown up before she made it down to breakfast and her breasts were painfully sensitive. It was as if every possible side effect of pregnancy was suddenly kicking in all at once. She had gone for her blood tests with Dr Silvano and he had reassured her that the results were normal.

Her nerves though were all over the place because Leo was due back that very evening and she was stressed out at the thought of seeing him again because he had been so polite and distant when he phoned. In addition, he had mentioned dining with Marina, who was also in London, and Grace had had to battle an innate streak of jealousy and tell herself that she was relaxed about his friendship with his former fiancée. But even so, Grace feared comparisons being made and knew it would always hurt that Leo should believe that Marina would have made him the ideal wife.

Josefina popped her head out of the French windows that led out to the terrace. 'Signora Zikos? Visitor. Meester Robert,' she pronounced, utilising her tiny English vocabulary.

Her brow pleating in surprise, for she didn't recognise the name, Grace stood up and stared at the man walking towards her, a chord of recognition striking her so hard that she froze and her eyes widened. The man was in his forties and of medium height with red hair as bright as her own. She had studied his photos on Facebook on several occasions and she knew who he was even though she couldn't quite credit that he could be in Italy to visit her.

'You're…' Grace began breathlessly.

'Tony Roberts, your father. I wanted to phone and warn you that I was coming but Leo was convinced it would be better if I simply surprised you,' he explained tautly. 'I hope he was right on that score…'

'Leo? You've *met* Leo?' Grace exclaimed, inviting the older man to sit down at the table she had vacated.

'He came to see me at the surgery last week and told me that you'd only recently found out what happened between your mother and I. By the way, I'm very sorry for your loss,' he told her with quiet sympathy. 'I wasn't sure this was the best time for me to meet you but your husband thought it might cheer you up.'

'My loss?' Grace repeated uncertainly, her brow indenting as she struggled to work out how such a misunderstanding could have taken place. 'But I didn't have a miscarriage…I'm still pregnant.'

Her father gave her a perplexed look, clearly confused.

'Did Leo tell you I had miscarried?' Grace

asked abruptly and when he nodded, everything fell into place for Grace and she finally realised that she had totally misinterpreted Leo's silence about her health and threatened miscarriage. Evidently, her text had gone astray and, having failed to receive it, Leo had assumed the worst and had then tactfully avoided any reference to pregnancy or babies. 'My goodness,' she whispered in shock, appalled to appreciate that Leo had been walking round London in ignorance of the reality that he was still going to be a father.

She explained the misunderstanding to her own father while trying to come to terms with the knowledge that, even divided as they currently were, Leo had still sought out her father and gone to see him for what could only be for her benefit.

'Are you saying that your husband *still* doesn't know that you didn't lose the baby?' he commented in consternation. 'You should go and phone him right now!'

'Leo's due back tonight and I'd prefer to tell him face to face,' Grace admitted with an abstracted smile, hoping that he would believe it was the very best news. 'I gather it was Leo who persuaded you to come to Italy and meet me?'

'I needed very little persuasion. I have waited over twenty years for this opportunity,' Tony Roberts pointed out with a wry smile. 'I assumed that you would hate me because your mother did. I didn't even know Keira had a brother in London. I never met any of her family because she didn't get on with them. I also had no idea that your mother had died when you were eleven. Had I known I would have asked if you could come and live with me instead of your aunt and uncle.'

Josefina brought out a tray of coffee and biscuits and Grace chatted to her father, satisfying her curiosity about his side of the family tree and asking about his three children and his wife. Tony had been so excited about the chance to meet his long-lost daughter that he had gone straight to his partners in the surgery where he worked and requested time off to fly straight out to Italy for the weekend. Grace was doubly touched, overwhelmed by her father's eagerness to meet her and stunned by the effort Leo had gone to on her behalf. Leo *cared* about her happiness, she realised, warmth filling her heart. Only a man who cared about her would have taken the trouble to set up such a meeting.

Morning coffee stretched into a leisurely lunch out on the terrace and the sunny afternoon sped past fast as father and daughter got to know each other, registering their similarities in outlook and interests with acceptance and pleasure. As the daylight faded, Tony took his leave, only then confiding that his wife, Jennifer, was waiting for him back at his hotel. Grace invited the couple to come for dinner the following evening and she watched the older man drive off in his hire car with genuine regret. She suspected that he would have been a lovely supportive father to have when she was younger and then she told herself off for concentrating once again on the negative rather than the positive. She decided it was wiser to be grateful for the enjoyable day she had spent in her father's company and was already looking forward to meeting her three younger half-siblings when she returned to London.

She prepared for Leo's return with care, donning a green dress with elaborate beadwork round the neckline and elegant heels. Hearing the helicopter come in to land, she breathed in deep and crossed her fingers for luck. He would probably still be angry with her because he hadn't received her text and she *had* behaved badly at the hospital. She was still brushing her hair when Leo entered the bedroom.

'I phoned Josefina and asked her to put dinner back an hour because I knew I was running late,' he told her, pausing directly in front of her to gaze down at her with shrewd dark golden eyes. 'How have you been?'

'Good, really good. Leo…I sent you a text from the hospital but I don't think you got it,' Grace said uncomfortably. 'I owe you an apology for some of the stuff I threw at you.'

'You were very distressed.'

'It wasn't the right time or place to spring all

that on you,' Grace muttered guiltily. 'I was in a bad frame of mind.'

'Understandably,' Leo cut in, stroking a long soothing forefinger along the taut line of her compressed lips. 'You're very tense. What's wrong?'

Grace backed away a few steps to clear her head. That close to Leo, her very skin prickling with awareness and the familiar scent of his cologne teasing her nostrils, she found it impossible to concentrate. 'If you'd got that text you'd have known that there's nothing wrong,' she told him with a wary half-smile. 'You were right and I was mistaken. I *was* being too pessimistic. The second scan picked up our baby's heartbeat the following morning.'

Leo froze, his ebony brows pleating in bewilderment. 'You mean…you're *saying*…?'

'That I'm still pregnant and everything looks fine. Feeling a bit sicker, mind you,' she burbled, suddenly shy beneath the burning intensity of his appraisal.

'You haven't lost the baby? *Truly?*' Leo pressed, striding forward, dark eyes alight like flames.

'Truly,' she whispered shakily as his arms closed tightly round her and she leant up against him for support. 'Sometimes I'm a terrible negative thinker, Leo. I only realised you didn't know about the baby when my father came to see me today. I thought possibly you hadn't mentioned the baby on the phone because you had changed your mind about certain things.'

'Well, I have changed my position on some stuff,' Leo stated in a driven undertone and then he startled her by swinging her up into his arms and spinning her round in a breathless rush. His charismatic grin lit up his lean dark features. 'That's the most wonderful news, *meli mou*! I didn't quite grasp how much I wanted our baby until I believed he was lost.'

'You're making me dizzy…put me down,' Grace urged, perspiration beading her short upper lip. With a groan of apology he settled her down at the foot of the bed where she lowered her head for a minute to overcome the nausea and dizziness the sudden spinning motion had induced.

'Are you all right?' Leo demanded, crouching at her feet and pushing up her face to see it. 'You are pale. I was an idiot. I just didn't think about what I was doing.'

Grace's nebulous fears about how Leo would react to her news had vanished. Leo was being so normal. There was no distance in him at all and he had been genuinely overjoyed to learn that she was still pregnant. That was not the reaction of a male who was considering the possibility of reclaiming his freedom with a divorce. Relief quivered through her slim, taut frame.

'I'm fine, Leo. I just get a little dizzy if I do anything too quickly. I've also been sick a couple of times,' she explained prosaically. 'It's like my body's finally woken up and realised it's pregnant.'

'It'll settle down,' Leo forecast cheerfully. 'How did things go with your father today?'

'What made you go and see him?' Grace asked instead.

'Well, I knew you wanted to meet him and I thought it would give you something else to think about,' he paraphrased a shade awkwardly. 'Grace—I've never felt so helpless in my life as when I believed you were losing our baby...'

'Me too...it wasn't something we could control.' Grace's fingertips stroked soothingly down his cheekbone to his strong jawline. 'All my worst instincts went into overdrive.'

Leo sprang lithely upright. 'No, I saw your point once I thought over what you'd said to me. I *did* make it all about the baby rather than about us. You could even say I used the baby as an excuse. Considering that I wanted you the very first moment I laid eyes on you and never stopped wanting you, I wasn't being honest with either of us.'

Her eyes widened at that admission. 'The very *first* moment?'

'It was like sticking my finger in an electrical socket,' Leo quipped. 'The attraction was instant and very powerful. I *had* to know you and then I *had* to have you. When I found myself wanting to hang onto you the morning after our night together, it freaked me out.'

'You did?' Grace was frowning. 'But we were only together one night.'

'One night with a very special woman who made me want much more from her than any woman I'd ever met,' Leo completed huskily. 'Why do you think I was too impatient to wait to hear from you afterwards? I was obsessed. I couldn't think of anything but seeing you again. It's a wonder I wasn't boiling bunnies...'

Grace was in shock but hanging onto his every word. 'Can't imagine that...but you said—'

'I said I didn't do love and then you threw me out of that hospital room when I badly needed to be with you and I had to get by without you for a week.'

'During which you suffered some sort of brainstorm?' Grace framed shakily.

'No, it finally hit me that I was *very* deeply attached to you and that it had just happened, regardless of all my doubts about such feelings.'

Grace finally stood up and approached him. '*Very* deeply attached?'

'Hopelessly,' Leo told her with his irresistible smile. 'Somewhere along the way I fell in love with you but I didn't recognise it. I knew I liked you, wanted you close and needed to look after you. I knew I was jealous of your friendship with Matt and very relieved when you didn't succumb to Bastien's legendary appeal. But I honestly did think that I was feeling all those things because it was natural for me to feel protective towards you when you were pregnant.'

'Easy mistake to make,' Grace told him breathlessly, unknotting his tie, yanking it free of his collar before embarking on his shirt buttons. 'You've just told me you love me and, since I love you too, we *should* be celebrating.'

'You love me? Even after all the mistakes I've made?' Leo pressed, stunning dark golden eyes locked to her flushed face and her huge beaming smile.

'Yes. Unlike you,' Grace murmured in unashamed one-upmanship, 'I never expected the man I married to be perfect.'

'But I *do* think you're perfect,' Leo argued heatedly. 'Absolutely perfect for me. You're beautiful and clever and warm and loving and you will make an absolutely brilliant mother.'

'Tell me more. My ego loves this,' Grace urged, laughing. 'I really should've guessed you loved me when you tracked down my father for me and got him out here. Instead I was too busy worrying about you dining out with Marina.'

Leo tensed. 'Why on earth would you worry about that?'

'Because you thought *she* was perfect and you were with her for *three* years.'

'If she'd been perfect for me I'd still have been with her and my sex drive would have centred on her,' Leo pointed out levelly. 'And Marina isn't perfect. Not only did she once have a one-night stand with my brother…'

'Bastien?' Grace pressed in surprise.

'Yes. She's also currently having an affair with a married man, although it is not quite as bad as it sounds,' Leo conceded reluctantly. 'His wife has been suffering from early onset dementia for years and is currently in a care home and recognising neither him nor his children. He's been living in limbo for a long time. You won't ever have to worry about my relationship with Marina. We're good friends and would be even better friends had we just settled for that.'

Grace smiled, accepting his explanation, putting those fears to rest. 'Why didn't you tell me that you were planning to look up my father?'

'I had to check Tony out first. He could have been hostile to an approach from you. He could have hurt your feelings and I couldn't have stood by and let that happen to you,' Leo assured her without apology. 'As it was I met him, liked him and saw quite a bit of you in him.'

'I did feel very comfortable with him.' Involuntarily, Grace's eyes flooded with tears and she rested her head down on Leo's shoulder with an apologetic sniff as she fought to regain control. Leo was so protective of her and after a lifetime of always having to look out for herself the depth of his caring and kindness meant a great deal to her. Yet once his managing ways had irritated the hell out of her, she acknowledged, marvelling at how much her outlook and his had changed since their first encounter. 'In the same way I've always felt comfortable with you.'

Leo lowered her back down to sit at the foot of the bed. 'Now for something very important that I skipped the first time around…' he husked, dropping down gracefully on one knee and lifting her hand. 'Grace Donovan…will you marry me?'

'Aren't we already married?' Grace breathed, taken aback and utterly mystified as he lifted her hand.

'Are we? Father Benedetto in the chapel in the village quite understands that you don't feel quite married after a civil ceremony and he has agreed to do the honours for us again,' Leo explained, deftly threading a ring onto her wedding finger. 'All we need to do is book our day.'

Her face the very picture of wonderment, Grace extended her hand, splaying her fingers the better to admire the breathtaking diamond cluster he had given her, and then she glanced down at the startling picture of Leo at her feet in romantic mode. 'I love the ring. Everything's happening backwards for us. We're getting engaged after we got married!'

'Better late than never,' Leo growled, springing back upright. 'You still haven't said yes—'

'Yes…yes…*yes*!' Grace carolled without hesitation, her sheer happiness bubbling over. 'Yes to marrying you, yes to another wedding, yes to loving you for the rest of my life!'

Leo tugged her gently up the bed and flattened her to the pillows. 'Do you think you can do that, *agapi mou*? I'm very far from being perfect.'

'Now that you know that, the sky's the limit in the improvement stakes,' Grace teased, wriggling as he skimmed her hair out of his path and claimed a scorching kiss that she felt all the way down to her curling toes. 'But you definitely don't need to improve at *this*…'

And Leo laughed and thought how shallow and empty his life had been before Grace and how much richer and more interesting it had become with her. As for Grace, she was much too busy getting Leo out of his shirt and admiring his muscular chest to think about anything.

Four years later, Grace stood on the deck of *Hellenic Lady*'s successor while her daughter Rosie played on deck with the family dog, a fluffy pug called Jonas. Grace was relaxed as she always was on such trips. She worked long hours as a doctor in the paediatrics department of a busy London hospital and cherished every day of her time off.

'Daddy…Daddy!' Grace spun round to watch her daughter throw herself boisterously at her father as he emerged from the main saloon.

Leo looked amazing in swim shorts, his lean, powerful body well-honed by exercise, black hair blowing in the breeze. They had enjoyed an incredibly busy four years together. Raising Rosie without a team of nannies would have been impossible with the hours Grace had been working while she trained in various hospitals, but since then, having attained a more settled working day, she had had the time to become a more hands-on mum. Rosie had Grace's red hair, Leo's rich dark eyes and skin that didn't burn in the sun the way her mother's did. She was a lively, affectionate child, happily attending nursery school.

Leo lowered his daughter to the deck and fought off the energetic advances of the dog. 'We'll be docking soon,' he reminded her with a lazy grin, stunning eyes straying appreciatively over the lush curves Grace had showcased in a blue bikini.

The heat of the Turkish sun was already beating down on Grace's bare shoulders and she lifted a towel to drape it round her and cover her skin, which never took a tan. They were returning to Marmaris to celebrate her twenty-ninth birthday at the Fever nightclub where they had first met. Anatole and her father's entire family were on board with them. She got on very well with her two adult half-brothers, who were students, and her little half-sister, who was still at school. From her stepmother, she had received the warm family acceptance that she had tried and failed to win from her uncle's family.

'I'll go and get changed.'

Leo banded an arm round her on the way down the stairs. 'How much of a hurry are you in?'

'It'll take me more than an hour to do my hair and get ready.'

Her husband dropped a kiss on the slope of her shoulder. 'Do you have an hour for me?'

Heat and anticipation shimmied through her. 'I've always got time for you,' she declared with an impish smile. 'You're a very demanding man.'

'But you like that about me, *agapi mou*,' Leo told her teasingly, closing the door of the master suite behind them.

And Grace had to admit, she did like that about him. They were very well-matched in the bedroom department, she acknowledged as he claimed a lingering blatantly sexual kiss that made her body hum and her heart thump with awareness. Being married to Leo was never bland or boring. He was everything she had ever dreamt of in a husband and she was blissfully happy with him.

'I was thinking…' Leo purred, extracting her from her bikini with skill while pausing to worship her full breasts and the sleek curve of her hips. 'Since we're on holiday and you're all mine night and day, do you think we should consider working on extending the family?'

'Jonas would probably love some company.'

Leo found the most ticklish spot on her entire body and punished her for that crack until she dissolved into laughter. 'You know very well I wasn't thinking of the dog!'

'Well, maybe I don't like you describing the conception of another child as work,' Grace countered tartly.

'Work I love, work I can never get enough of, you maddening woman,' Leo groaned into the fall of her hair. 'You know I'm crazy about you, don't you?'

Grace fingered the flawless diamond pendant at her throat, which he had given her for her birthday, and smiled. 'The suspicion has crossed my mind once or twice.'

'Rosie is like a mini you and I'd love another one.'

'I'll put my pills away,' Grace murmured with amusement, linking her arms round his strong brown neck, appreciating his lean, darkly handsome features and his gorgeous eyes. 'I love you, Leo.'

'Nowhere near as much as I love you, *agapi mou*,' Leo countered.

'You're always so competitive,' she complained without great heat as she arched into the hard strength of his body and let her senses sing to the sensual magic of his demanding mouth.

* * * * *

MILLS & BOON®

Large Print – December 2015

The Greek Demands His Heir
Lynne Graham

The Sinner's Marriage Redemption
Annie West

His Sicilian Cinderella
Carol Marinelli

Captivated by the Greek
Julia James

The Perfect Cazorla Wife
Michelle Smart

Claimed for His Duty
Tara Pammi

The Marakaios Baby
Kate Hewitt

Return of the Italian Tycoon
Jennifer Faye

His Unforgettable Fiancée
Teresa Carpenter

Hired by the Brooding Billionaire
Kandy Shepherd

A Will, a Wish...a Proposal
Jessica Gilmore

1115 Rom LP